THE CROWN
OF OMENS

A Blood and Steel Saga Story

E J Doble

Also by E J Doble:

THE BLOOD AND STEEL SAGA
The Crown of Omens
1: *The Fangs of War*
2: *The Horns of Grief*

REALM OF THE PROPHETS
1: *The Crescent Moon*

GRIMDARK FAIRYTALES
1: *Gold, Lock and Key*

Cover art, design and illustration by: @diego_spezzoni
Map illustration by: @jogbrogzin

Dedicated to Diego Spezzoni.

For being a fantastic illustrator,
and a friend.

Welcome to

The Blood and Steel Saga

This book forms an entrance-point into the cruel and violent world of the Icebreaker Sea: a place of ruin and greed, where an imperial power and its former colony stand at the brink of a war fifty-years in the making. It is a conflict that will consume everything, inflicting death upon thousands and upending the lives of thousands more. It is a war of gods and men, vying for the heirship of a power greater than any can imagine.

It is a war with no winners, to control the balance of the Known World.

This book tells the story of the single, fateful night where it all began, taken from the perspectives of ten unique figures and their tumultuous, interwoven lives. This book is an illustration of the world at large and the people that occupy it; it is a demonstration of the violence to come, and the scars it will inflict along the way.

So welcome, one and all, to *The Blood and Steel Saga*.

You have been warned...

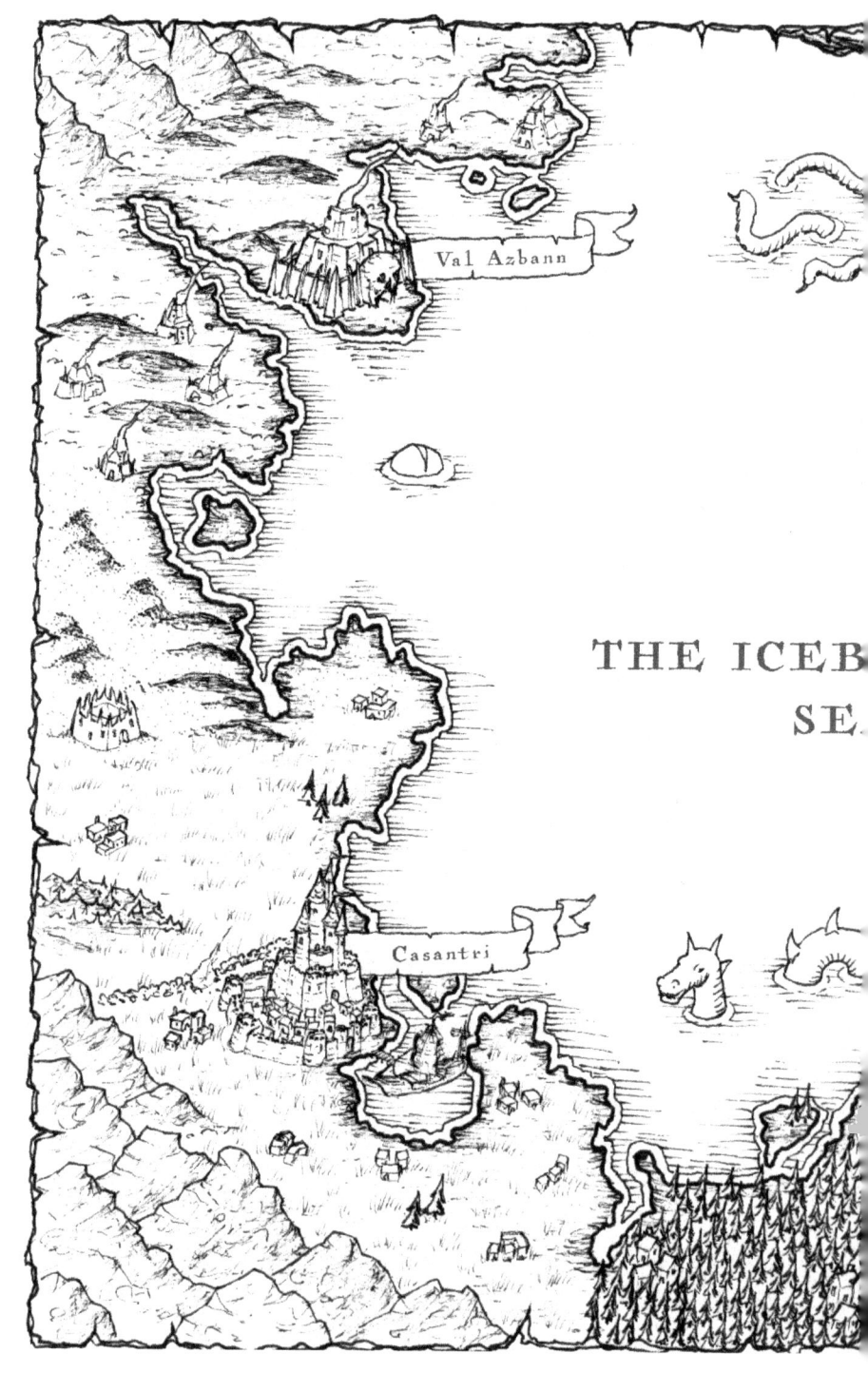

Val Azbann

THE ICEB

SE.

Casantri

EAKER

City of the Sun

"When the sun bleeds, and dusk sets,
the king will die come morning;
By the swallow's song, adrift to the wind,
Hear the bells come knocking.
To cannon blasts and tyrant shadows,
Heed the cries of the faithless few
Who drive the blades and fletch the arrows
And churn the world anew.
The sins of the fathers make torment the sons,
Mark them all for breaking;
When the sun bleeds and dusk sets,
Their undoing be of their own
Making."

12-1, VII.I
"The Tale of Ruinenonn"

The Tower

The moon rose from the east that night, passing overhead in silence, bathing the harbourside in streaks of white like the pearly scales of a fish. The slate rooftops of the vast storehouses glistened by the city's outer walls; the huge wooden cranes used to pull cargo from ships stood like spears in the depths of night. The tiny dockworkers, milling about like ants, hefted torches and shifted down the many cobbled paths with a dutiful purpose in their step. They were the single occupants of the harbourside that night. Silence was their only friend.

Out to sea, the lapping waves pulled in across the bay, rippling out from the vastness beyond and disappearing altogether. Pontoons dotted the harbour walls, stretching out into the deeper waters like bony fingers, with tiny fishing boats moored to their pillars. To the south, larger galleons sat anchored in the dark, stood as tall as the distant mountains under the cold moonlight. Workers trickled up and down their gangplanks, loading supplies into their hulls, readying for the next call to arms when the ships would set sail once more. Heading out into the impossible dark, on course for danger and ruin.

Out into the expanse of the Icebreaker Sea, at the behest of their ancient king.

"Mist is pretty heavy today… can't even see the Carrhonn Isles, it's so thick."

"I don't imagine they can see much from the headland in the north, either. Sky o'er there looks like soup."

"Must be mighty eerie being in that old tower when the weather's like this. Wouldn't want it to be me."

"Not that our tower 'ere is much better, that is, but at least we can see *something*…"

In a watchtower, stood like a black sentinel at the harbour wall, two guards peered out of a top-storey window towards the headland in the north, which lay engulfed in a thick blanket of sea mist. The entire hillside and surrounding cliffs – from the rocky crags to the lush Provencian plains – had been submerged, cutting off all visibility across the coast. The north-most wall of the harbour, jutting up with dagger-like turrets in the dark, was the last thing either of the guards could see before the mist shrouded everything from view, and the wider world became lost to the night. It was ominous, almost, to look out on the moonlit sea like that.

An omen, perhaps, if one dared call it so.

In the watchtower, one of the guards – with a paunchy belly and a thick head of ginger hair – looked from the grey headland in the north down to the lapping water far beneath them, and sneered.

Just another night like any other: no need to jump at shadows.

Rolling his tongue across his teeth, he launched a gobbet of spit into the air and watched its arcing passage down towards the sea, smirking to himself with a quiet satisfaction—

Or that was, until he looked up at his colleague – a chiselled woman with a strong jaw and rings around her fingers – and saw her frowning at him in disgust.

"What?" he grumbled scratching his stomach.

"What was that?" she replied, her eyes following the arc his spit had taken.

"I dunno… had a bit o' phlegm, was all. Had to bring it up an' get it out."

"That's gross."

He scoffed. "There are far worse things in life than a bit o' phlegm, y'know. Far worse."

"Well yea… I mean, staring at your ugly chops four nights a week is quite a distasteful prospect, if we're being honest."

He put a hand to his chest, faking offense. "How *rude*."

"I would say I cared, but… well, the truth hurts sometimes, y'know? Or is that fact a bit harder to '*bring up and get out*'?" She grinned facetiously.

He rolled his eyes, trying not to show his amusement. "Fuck yourself," he exclaimed.

"You're *most* welcome." She smirked, and then waved her hand in dismissal. "But anyway, enough of that… there's something more important to discuss." The woman turned and sat on a wooden stool next to her, with a neat incision down the middle of her face where the moonlight and shadow met. She reached down to her side and eased something out of her satchel, resting it on her knees and looking up to the ginger man with a twinkle in her eye. "I've been meaning to show you something, that I recently ordered through the Munitions Guild: it's something that I think you'll find quite *interesting*, knowing what you're like…"

The guard's eyes seemed to pop from their sockets.

"I… yea…"

Looking at the item in her lap with his mouth agape, the guard hardly registered what she had said. He hardly comprehended the world at all, in fact. His brain was awash with intrigue and shock, lowering down to a crouch almost automatically.

You lucky son of a bitch…

It was a crossbow, freshly manufactured by the smiths in the Munitions Guild, with a polished oak frame and a loading column of the finest Provencian steel. The winding mechanisms were radiant under the light of the moon, oiled and intricately placed in the weapon's limber frame. Looking upon it then in all its unblemished beauty, he couldn't help but marvel at its design.

"It's… remarkable," was all he managed to say in the end, hiding his envy behind a mask of joy. "How did you come by this?"

"I had a bit o' coin left over from the expeditions I did during the sun months, hunting bandits out on the plains to the south," she explained, lifting the weapon to study it herself. "And as it so happened, I had just enough saved up to purchase one of these newer models from the Munitions Guild… with a guardsman's discount, of course." She scoffed. "I dread to think what this would cost for a hunter or a mercenary."

"Not that those frightful bastards need any more efficient means of killing people," he replied, screwing his nose up at the thought. "And not that they would take great care of such an… *exquisite* weapon."

She nodded, smiling. "My thoughts exactly."

"So… how much did it set you back, in the end?"

"This one cost thirteen gold pieces to the mark, and not a silver round less."

He gulped, pulling at his collar with a flush of heat. *That's more'n I make in a quarter-year.* "Quite an expense, then, ay?"

"It was, yea… but luckily I was paid well doing the expeditions, so I didn't end up losing out too badly… hardly made a *dent,* in fact," she replied. The edge of her mouth curled up slightly, placing the weapon back on her legs, and he sensed the dripping smugness in her voice. She was proud and somewhat prideful, and an uncomfortable heat rose in his neck as he realised exactly why she was showing him the weapon in the first place.

She's gloating, he registered, with a sourness in his mouth. *She knows I could ne'er afford such a weapon on a guard's pay… and I don't have the wherewithal for the expeditions anymore to even consider getting one on the future.* As a memory resurfaced, a nagging pain twisted through his left knee and forced him to squint. He adjusted it slowly, stretching his joint, and released the tension with a long sigh. *I'm not the fighter I used to be, that's for sure.*

But I know a damn-sight more than smug bastards like you, he grumbled, finally meeting her eye again. The petty arrogance swimming there was enough to make him sneer. *You'd do well to respect your elders, and keep your pride in check.*

I wish I had when I was your age——

"Would you like to hold it?" she said suddenly, lifting her eyebrows. "I don't mind, y'know. It may be a fine piece, but I'm not that precious about it if you did want to handle it."

He frowned at her, suddenly caught off-guard. *Why has she asked me that?* He puzzling over her question like a child with a new toy: wondering what he was missing, and why she'd asked at all.

And he didn't get to reach much of a conclusion, in the end, as the crossbow was near-enough dropped in his hands, and he fumbled to keep hold of it in his large, meaty hands.

"Well, um… thank you," he exclaimed, adjusting his grip on the frame. "It's, uh… it's *light*."

"It is, isn't it?"

"I've never held a weapon with this kind o' balance."

"Really? Well… how about that," she mused. "I mean… I don't really understand how they make it so light, to be honest. It must be the wood, or something…"

She gave a fake laugh, brushing her hair with her fingers; he bristled, clasping the crossbow grip tighter. *You're feigning ignorance, aren't you?* he accused. *You already know… you know full fucking well how it's made and why it's light. Of course it's the fucking wood. It's how it's designed, for Mother's sake, you irritating, feckless—*

"Yea… must be the wood," he replied, smiling softly. "Oak, is it?"

"*Carbol,* actually. From Rodenia."

"Ah." He grimaced. "Very… *elegant*."

"Yes, *very* elegant indeed."

Ignoring her, the guard turned back to the open window again and looked out on the wall of sea mist. He lifted the crossbow as if ready to fire, imagining her head somewhere in the crosshair.

Makes my blood boil, that one does.

He took several deep breaths, holding them for a moment each time, as he scanned across the headland to the north. Tracing the gloom and the grey, he passed across to the vast waters beyond, following the roll of the waves and the curling shapes of the mist—

When his eyes stopped.

And his mind stopped.

And every conscious thought ceased to be suddenly.

Sweat pulled over his palms and up his spine. Shivers rippled up his arms. His pulse raced, as he lowered the crossbow to his side.

"Um, there... there are..." he spluttered, losing sensation in his tongue.

Absently, he turned to his colleague, pale as a wraith with trembling jowls, and extended his finger towards the distant sea—

"*...ships approaching...*"

Staring at him – through him, even – the woman's eyes swam with colour suddenly, the colour leeching from her skin. She lifted from her seat, scraping the stool legs over the stone, and looked out the oval window into the bay beyond. She followed the guard's direction out across the waves beyond.

To find something unimaginable at the end of it, that plunged her heart through the floor.

There were black bowsprits emerging from the mist. Black sails on black masts, with black rigging and black bows and the tiny dots of fires scattered over their decks. Pulling out from the gloom, into the moonlight of the open harbour. A dozen of them, at least, surging over the waves, turning at the outskirts of the mist to face the city with their broadsides. Darkness clouding them, following them everywhere, spinning with the vapour and churning with the waves. They were death and they were shadow.

Silent bastions of horror, appearing before their very eyes.

"What... what is this? What... what's... going on?" the woman muttered, shedding her confidence to reveal a tired little girl way in over her head. "What the *fuck* is going on!"

"I don't know!" he bellowed in reply, sweat beading down his forehead. "I don't know, it's... I..."

"Those aren't our ships. They aren't ours. They aren't..." She heaved air into her lungs, blinking heavily. Violent shakes crawled over her hands. "We need to warn someone, we... we have to get out, go and tell the—"

"There's no time! They're already here. By the time we get word out, it'll—"

He stopped.

He stared.

His words fell short and his lips fell closed—

As a blast of cannons ruptured the night air, and the entire bay before them exploded with orange flame.

Black shot poured across the skies towards them. Chain-shot whistled with the wind. Mortars bellowed like thunder and fizzed up through the clouds. Yellow fire and orange fire and grey smoke twisted in the mist, spiralling into the stars—

A massive vibration swept out over the waves and shook the watchtower on its foundations, bellowing like thunder. The deafening crackle of the cannon blasts burst the two guards' ears and nearly toppled them backwards. They grappled the edge of the window to hold steady, swaying violently, looking out on the horror that awaited them, flying through the air like a volley of arrows—

It was impossible. It couldn't happen. It couldn't be.

It can't be...

The ginger guard stood there, wide-eyed and fearful with a crossbow in his hands, watching the shot chase over the waves toward them at frightening speed – tracing the path of a singular cannonball against the light of the moon, spiralling towards the base of their tower with perfect, fatal precision.

There was no moment to be spared, in the end. There was not even a whisper of a prayer.

The guard blinked once; the woman screamed.

And the entire tower exploded beneath them.

II

The Cannon

The cannonball impacted the base of the tower with a crack like shattering plates, and his eyes seemed to swell in their sockets at the sight of it.

The massive stone blocks caved in effortlessly, crumbling foundations that had stood for centuries unopposed. The top half of the watchtower seemed to slide off its base, decapitated by the force of the attack, swallowing itself as it fell. The entire structure toppled forward, slipping from the harbour wall in one great column of broken stone. The Tarrazi soldiers aboard the black ship around him held their breaths, watching it fall one piece at a time.

And when the *thud* of the massive tower hitting the water finally rippled across the bay, an almighty cheer went up amongst his kin, as they slapped their forearms and invoked their gods with an almost feverish pride. They revelled in it, savouring every breath. It was intense and it was powerful and it was mighty.

And he couldn't believe what he had just done.

The Tarrazi boy, stood at the centre of it all – with the smoking cannon at his side and the striking stick in his hand –found his words had abandoned him altogether. He was frozen to the spot, his eyes locked on the remains of the tower opposite, his skin burning from the coursing winds and the salty spray dashing his face.

At his back, beyond the numb ringing in his ears from the blast, he could hear soldiers cheering his name and trying to get his attention, full of jubilance and pride. Soldiers grabbed his shoulders and shook him – patting his head like a dog – remarking of his skill and how the gods smiled upon him, despite the fact he was only seventeen-winter's old. Euphoria swept across the ship in great waves around him, like the faces of his parents on his Proving Day – but, in that fractious moment, he couldn't bring himself to realise it. He had seized up, claimed by the shadows, looking out on the harbourside in disbelief.

Wondering what he had begun.

Looking to his left, tracing the grey smudge of the harbour wall, he watched the destruction unravel in the dark with flashes of gold and red, as the other cannon shots reached the harbourside and tore through everything in their path. Stacks of boxes exploded in shrapnel and dust; spindly loading cranes snapped down their middles and spiralled into the watery abyss; watchtowers and barracks were buffeted by lead rounds, collapsing in on themselves with the screams of the dying inside. A wooden pontoon veered to one side as its supporting pillars snapped, sending the whole thing down into the murky waters beneath. A watchtower had its top-most level torn open by a barrage, showering massive stone blocks on unsuspecting dock workers fleeing the scene just below. A lone soldier, stood at the end of the nearest pontoon with a torch to-hand, took a chain-shot to the neck, and the Tarrazi boy could do nothing but watch as the man's head tore from his neck in a spurting arc of blood.

A shiver crept down his spine; sickness swam in his throat.

Az-kabza—

"To arms, *feduzak,* to arms!" came a loud cry from the stern, rising up over the din of voices and scraping feet. "Cannons, *now*!"

The boy glanced back for a moment, following the voice, and saw the imposing shape of a black-armoured figure occupying the stern of the ship. The moonlight shone painfully behind them, so their body was little more than a shadow, and their earless head stood atop their neck like a cannonball. The young Tarrazi stared at them for some moments, lost in a trance of fear and wonder, before someone shoved against his shoulder and he snapped back to reality, turning to the dead cannon at his side.

Cannons... ready...

Pressing his hand against the base of the barrel, he ground his teeth and inched the cannon forward slowly, hissing at the scolding pains over his fingers where the ignition powder had detonated inside. Redness blemished across his palms; as he wheeled the cannon into position, he peeled his hands away to find them steaming, doused with sea spray and burning with salt.

His eyes watered as he strained his forearms, holding his hands before him as in prayer, whimpering quietly to himself—

As a hand cuffed him across the back of his head, slapping the bald skin beneath his braid with enough force to nearly topple him over.

The immediate shock was overwhelming. His skin crawled with rawness. For a fractious moment, he thought he'd been killed.

He looked back behind him – wide-eyed and angry and hating of all things – and was about to curse whoever had done it to him—

When he spied the huge man from the stern striding past, cuffing another soldier around the back of the head with a ferocious snarl.

The young Tarrazi shrunk away with a gasp almost immediately, acknowledging his fear. He turned back to the cannon and averted his eyes, offering a quiet apology to the gods – watching as the ship swayed and his stomach churned and his hands shuddered furiously.

Must obey... must obey...

Returning to the task at hand, he struggled with removing the cannon's thick fuse like a child trying to navigate a door-handle, pulling and clutching and hissing in the dark with no dexterity in his fingers. He pulled the old fuse away after some time and threw it out into the sea, where the chopping waters and thrashing waves swallowed it whole.

Shivering in the wind, he prized a fresh fuse from a holster on his belt and rolled it between his fingers, breathing and biting with eyes like shiny black orbs. Under the shaky moonlight he tried to jam it back into the hole where he had removed the other fuse, fumbling stupidly with it. His fingers were numb, impossibly numb, prying at the fuse chamber like pieces of seaweed. A deep pain ran through his knees, holding steady on the rocking vessel as the waves grew more violent beneath. He gulped down great lengths of air, the cannon so slippery beneath his fingers—

Until the fuse locked into place at last, and he pulled his hands away.

He released a shaky breath, blinking heavily into the wind.

Perhaps hope… after all.

He acknowledged his handiwork with a nod, assessing the position of the cannon, before turning around—

To have a cannonball shoved into his hands by one of the shipmates, which he nearly dropped on his toes with the force of it.

Grimacing – glaring at the worker who had thrown the cannonball at him – he moved back towards his cannon and slid the ball into a hatch on the upper barrel, wiping the sticky ignition powder off of his hands as he did so. It stank of burnt ash and open wounds; he grappled the handle to the hatch and sealed it closed, locking the cannonball and its horrific smell in place. His nausea seemed to balloon because of it, with the residue burning the hairs in his nostrils.

And his hands just wouldn't stop shaking—

"Make ready!" a thunderous voice bellowed from the prow, lifting a tight-fisted gauntlet into the air as a wave of sea-spray showered the deck. "Make ready, *feduzak!*"

Scratching wood and metal clawed at the boy's ears suddenly, pervading all other sense. The cannons next to him were rolled into position, grinding against their stoppers. Their barrels pointed through the hatches in the ship's hull like the muzzles of hungry Hounds. The other soldiers on deck – all so much older than him, so fearless – slid the striking sticks from their waistbands and bared their teeth, ready for action.

The young Tarrazi watched them in silence, with a terror chilling him to his bones. He watched them, mirrored on either side, on every ship across the bay as far as the eye could see—

He felt so small. Their pride was his unease; their blood-lust was his fear. He never understood it. He was so lost and so alone, in the depths of night so far from home on a ship he had never seen before in a place he had only heard of in his nightmares. He felt so young and so lost, in the end.

"You go to war, skal," his trainer had said in the recruitment camp, many moons ago. He had been carving the end of a stick into a spear, watching the wood chips scatter over the earth. *"War… it is like nothing you have ever known. Death will be your shadow there, skal…*

"Only blood and steel awaits you——"

A trumpet blast erupted in his ears suddenly, echoing off into the night.

He rubbed his head——

"Aim your cannons!" the huge Tarrazi roared from the prow, gritting his teeth in a lustful glee.

The crunch and grind of cannons buffeted him from both sides, cranking and locking into place. He looked down on his own weapon for a moment in a daze, all of his training abandoning him as he thought back to his homeland, and his mother's face and his father's strong smile and the sun beating down on the small green rivers by his village. Thinking of everything in that fragile moment; remembering nothing, in the end.

He lowered his striking stick to the fuse; a tear laced down his cheek.

I want to go home——

"FIRE!"

The striking stick scraped across the cannon's barrel, showering the fuse in sparks as it fizzed and spat and coiled its way down into the body of the cannon——

A hissing like a serpent echoed from within for a few heartbeats after, as the ignition powder——

BOOM.

…orange fire.

…ash.

…smoke.

…detonation…

Tearing at his ears, at his eyes. Burning his throat.

Rippling down the rank, over a hundred of them firing, launching death into the night sky.

Orange.

Grey.

Crimson fire.

He gasped and shivered. He tried to shy away, to get away from it all.

He lifted his hands to head—

A huge wave slapped against the port side of the ship, throwing him against the railing next to the cannon and knocking all the air from his lungs.

He shuddered. His skin crawled. A string of vomit splattered through his teeth and spewed down into the sea below.

His eyes bulged in their sockets; he looked up with panting breaths to the harbourside opposite them.

Witnessing there another wave of destruction, tearing across the horizon.

He wasn't even sure where his shot had landed – he wasn't even sure if his cannon had fired, even. Instead, his focus lay on the toppled watchtower he had destroyed on the first barrage, as a hail of shots tore through a warehouse behind, and the audible creak and crunch of sliding beams rippled like thunder. The entire building collapsed on its side, tearing itself open completely, killing a small band of soldiers approaching the harbourfront on a path nearby.

Further to the south, a wide thoroughfare of stalls and cargo formed a path from the dock to the city wall, which stood ominously in the background like a serpent's scales. Several stray shots hurtled through the open air there, smashing the small market to pieces, impacting the wall behind with a horrific *thud* of stone that reverberated through the whole city beyond. The wall remained standing in spite of it, shaking off the attacks with a sturdy defiance, but the cracks that the cannon-shot had inflicted glistened like scars under the moon, offering reminders to anyone who dared look of the destruction the Tarrazi were causing.

And still he watched on, pinned to the railing of the ship with horror in his eyes, as shot after shot rained down on the harbourside, obliterating everything in its path. The moonlight faded and brightened in the sky above; clouds swirled and waves crashed, salt and static lathering the air. His white knuckles clenched the wood beneath him, frozen in place, swaying aboard the vessel with nowhere else to go—

An orange light like dragon's breath swam across his vision in the south suddenly, followed by a tremendous *boom* that flushed the sails above.

He looked there in awe as a curious child would, not expecting the horrors that would follow.

What was tha—

A storehouse went up in flames behind several other buildings, the explosion rocketing skyward in a vast plume of ochre and crimson. Ash and dust billowed out in all directions, mixing with the sea mist and the clouds high above. Debris were thrown across the harbour, scattering over the waters beneath in a frenzy and impaling anyone unfortunate enough to lie in its path.

The entire dock seemed to sway on its foundations, swimming suddenly with light. It flickered in his eyes like a candle, painting a destructive image in his mind that he could never let go. Spilling over the city walls; climbing the masts of the distant enemy ships—

That had now shifted from their docks, silent as ghosts in the night, and glided delicately towards the Tarrazi.

He gasped.

Shuddered.

His heart pierced against his ribs.

They have… turned away…

He craned his neck past the other ships.

His hands trembled against the railing—

They're coming for us...

Desperation flooded him with a wash of adrenaline, all fear and grief and sorrow.

Looking to the other soldiers on the ship – who delighted at the violence that seemed to consume the harbour – he realised that he was the only one who had seen what was approaching from the south: the massive behemoths barrelling over the waves, readying their cannons, channelling straight toward them in an arrowhead through the dark.

They were huge. Impossibly huge.

Dark and foul and fatal—

A heartbeat passed.

The young Tarrazi lost control of his mind—

And all he could think to do, in the end, was scream.

He didn't hear his own words, as the petrified sound left his lips. He didn't hear any noise at all, in fact, beyond the thrashing of waves and the billowing wind. It was all just sound, and pain.

It seemed never-ending—

His throat scratched. Sea water sprayed over his skin. His chest curled in, straining against his ribs as his scream grew louder—

There were other voices in his ears suddenly; the soldiers turned to him like puppets. Confused, at first, but forming a realisation soon after.

They turned to the prow, looking from the huge figure in the black armour to the line of boats across the bay. Scanning along them; looking on further to the horizon. Watchful and waiting, assessing the scene—

Clutching the railing in horror, as they spied enemy ships turning from the docks towards them, their double-level broadsides flashing like knives in the perilous, fatal dark—

The boy wasn't sure how long had passed since he first screamed. It was both a heartbeat and an eternity, meshed into one.

But as his lips fell closed, and another tear streaked his cheek, a warning cry called out from the prow of the ship that shivered down his spine, and the wood-panel floor seemed to rot at his feet, preparing to swallow him whole.

"ZOLTHA SHIPS! EVERYBODY DOWN!"

His knees buckled, throwing him down against the deck with a slap of seawater as a massive, thunderous *boom* ripped across the harbourside towards them—

Whistling rounds clipped the skies above.

Cracking hulls and snapping masts followed.

Bloody screams; splashing and screeching.

Cries and commands, voices hoarse and damning.

The boat rocked around him, scudding on the waves. Splashes from impacts sounded somewhere in the waters in front of him, dangerously close to their vessel. He held his breath and whispered a prayer, remembering how proud his mother had been of him for going out there and fighting for his people.

He didn't feel very proud anymore.

The enemy volley finished almost as quickly as it had begun, as the last of the metal rounds peppered the sea and sunk to their murky graves.

The young Tarrazi exhaled and lifted his head fearfully, spying other soldiers doing the same – but before he got a chance to assess the damages aboard the other Tarrazi ships, or to see if the enemy vessels were planning another attack, a second cry hailed from the prow of the ship, where the soldier in the black armour swayed to a stand and snarled at the harbour nearby.

"Open out the sails!" they bellowed, jolting their arm toward the nearest wooden pontoon. "Prepare to disembark, *now*!"

Disembark? The young Tarrazi stood and swayed in disbelief, his stomach in his throat. He looked from the huge figure at the prow to the wooden pontoon nearby.

What mean... disembark...

His answer came with a flush of unfurling sails above him, and a jolt of speed that took the ship forward and threw the entire deck off its axis.

The young Tarrazi spilled backwards, slipping on the watery panels underfoot. His legs went out from under him, as he toppled back and crashed against the opposing cannon, cracking his spine over the barrel with an audible wail of pain—

A cranking sound echoed out from the stern somewhere behind him: the whole ship swung right with a massive hail of seawater, cutting across the waves with ferocious momentum.

The boy scraped his nails across the cannon barrel at his back, scrabbling for purchase, clawing for dear life as the wind lashed over his face—

The ship levelled out again, heading directly for the harbourside and the wooden pontoon—

He lost all grip, throwing himself into the starboard railing, pushing more sick into his mouth that he spluttered and coughed through blindly.

Snot dripped from his nose. Tears lashed his eyes. He snorted and wheezed uncontrollably, crying out for his mum and his home and his bed: all comforting things he could never have, and would never know again, on the back of a ship in a horrible place he didn't understand, for reasons he would never know—

A pair of hands gripped his shoulders, pulling him away from the railing and turning him round to face the wider deck.

The young Tarrazi squinted into the moonlight, his face a mess of wrinkles and tears, mouth gawping like a frog trying its luck catching flies—

As the huge soldier from the prow looked down on him with disgust, lifting a hand to clamp his jaw and jam his mouth shut.

The boy's sobbing ceased almost immediately. His skin crawled and his back seized up. The shimmering orbs of his eyes stared blindly at the figure opposite: the black marks under their eyes; the deep red gums pulled back in a snarl; the knot of scars across the left side of their face, carving up around their earless scalp. The powerful grip on his mouth disabled him entirely, caught in the clutches of a being most foul. The young Tarrazi didn't even swallow, for fear of the wrath that might come. He didn't breathe, nor blink. The figure stood opposite him in silence, their teeth like sharpened fangs, with the scene of a great battle playing out just behind them, between the greatest navies of the Known World. But the boy dared not look, or even glance that way.

And something told him his life depended on it.

The huge soldier relinquished their grip a few heartbeats later, dropping him onto shaky legs with hardly any strength to spare. Reaching down to their side, the soldier pulled something into the light and shoved it against the boy's chest, which he wrapped his arms around and held tight against his sternum.

And it was only when the figure in the armour turned and paced away, that the young Tarrazi realised he'd just been given a sword.

"We approach the dock!" the soldier bellowed, marching down the middle of the deck, unsheathing his weapon. "Make ready to disembark!"

The young Tarrazi stared at the weapon in his hands and sensed a great weight press down across his back, as if one of the gods had come down and squat him under Their thumb. He unsheathed the blade, throwing the leather holster to the floor, and studied its beautiful, silent iridescence, dancing under the moon like a shooting star. He had never held a true blade before. He had never thought he would need to. The wooden practice weapons he had sparred with back home were like ugly spoons compared to the delicateness that lay in his hands then. He had only ever seen them, imagined them – he had been told to fear them, above all else, for the inevitability they held.

"A blade... a good thing," his trainer had explained, as they cut a tiny mark in their fingertip and watched the dark blood trickle out. *"But every blade that emerges, leaves this world marked with blood. That is the curse of the sword...*

"As you will one day find out—"

"GANGPLANKS READY!"

He looked around suddenly, snapping from his trance, and saw the other soldiers along the portside with swords glinting in their hands. They wore grins like plastered clay, with hungry eyes and frightful howls. Some donned great black helmets, while others fastened themselves into shoulder guards and greaves. They appeared menacing in the twilight: denizens of the gods, ready to exact Their will on the world and unleash Their wrath. He looked upon them, bunching up as the gangplanks were raised in preparation for landing, and wondered where he had gone so wrong to end up in such company.

I don't... I...

The sails billowed overhead, drawing together as the winches screeched and the vessel slowed and the rudder creaked somewhere in the murk beneath them. In the distance – in a far off place he wanted no part of – the orange glows and thundering blasts of cannon-fire reigned down across the bay, the ships launching at each other in a dogged frenzy, trying desperately to stay alive. He saw showers of splintered wood and plumes of black smoke against the haze of orange flame. The percussive blasts reverberated through his ears, even from that distance, as volleys of shot continued to blast the harbourside and destroy everything they could. It was anarchy and it was pain; it was vengeance and it was ruin.

He saw it all, unravelling before him like the black sails above, and found he couldn't speak.

What have we done...

The black vessel coasted against the pontoon and drew to a stop. The gangplanks slapped down onto the wooden beams, accompanied by the sounds of thudding feet as the soldiers piled off the ship, with the mighty bellows of their leader at their backs spurring them on.

The young Tarrazi stumbled forward, approaching the last soldier who wobbled precariously down the plank, leaping onto the pontoon and charging off with the rest.

Perhaps... I live, he thought quietly, placing a foot on the gangplank and testing his balance. *Perhaps I live... go home one day.*

He stepped from the ship's deck, looking down to see the churning waves lapping up against the hull, seething with the pale bodies of flesh-eating fish. A bubble formed in his throat, which he swallowed down painfully.

This is it.

He thought of his mother and his father, and his village. He thought of home, and his life before.

He took another step, conquering his fears.

A deep breath filled his lungs.

This is where it——

The Bowstring

The arrow arced through the sky and pierced the Tarrazi in the side of the neck, burrowing through into their collarbone over the lip of their armour. It stopped them in their tracks, teetering precariously on the gangplank between the boat and the pontoon; they pawed at the blood that gushed from their neck in a sudden, fatal stream. The sword fell from their hand, spinning end-over-end into the churning waters below.

And no sooner had it hit the surface, than the Tarrazi fell too, plummeting down toward a murky grave and the teeth of flesh-eating fish.

At the harbour wall at the end of the pontoon, with the waves lapping up against the stone beneath her, the Casantri archer lowered her weapon and released a tempestuous sigh, watching the waters seethe beneath the pontoon as the monsters gorged on their flesh. It was no small mercy that the soldier had probably died before they hit the waters below. It was testament to her skill that they had been killed outright in the first place.

Because the idea of being eaten alive by giant lampreys isn't one I'd wish on any mortal soul, she admitted, curling her nose up.

Even if they are just some pale freak.

"That was a great shot!" another archer called out next to her, loosing his own arrow into the crush of Tarrazi streaming down the pontoon towards them. "Right in the neck!"

"We've still got work to do, though," she replied absently, tearing her eyes from the churning water. "They're comin' at us fast!"

She squat down behind a stack of boxes and slid an arrow free of her quiver, lacing it between her fingers like a sewing needle. It was an old trick her mother had taught her long ago, on the open plains to the west where she had grown up and practiced various crafts: drawing arrows from pouches; tanning leather on a wooden rack; tying fish hooks to tiny pieces of twine. They were all delicate, measured skills, requiring much time and patience. And even though she had long abandoned tanning, and wasn't much use with a fishing pole anymore, there was still a pleasing warmth in her chest when she knocked an arrow against her bowstring and slid it in place, imagining her mother's warm smile next to her.

She found herself smiling too.

How I wish you could see me now, ma.

She drew in a long breath and peered over the stack of boxes, scanning the faces of the Tarrazi charging down the pontoon ahead. They were a terrifying people to behold, she admitted: with pale skin like glass, and black eyes and red gums and earless skulls like tumours. They were muscular and formidable. The wooden panels at their feet creaked and strained under their weight. Half of them wore armour; the other half carried shimmering steel swords as long as their arms, glinting in the twilight. Their numbers had depleted significantly since they had landed, with four other archers alongside her pummelling them with arrows – but even so, she questioned whether their combined defence would be enough to hold them back.

We can but hope…

With a snarl, she stood and loosed her arrow into the throng, watching it zip past a massive suit of armour and impale another Tarrazi in the eye, stopping them in their tracks.

A roar went up from the other archers as the Tarrazi collapsed and was swallowed by the crush of bodies behind. She didn't see what became of them – she was too busy ascertaining her next target, sliding another arrow onto the bowstring – but the distinct thud-and-slap of a body sliding off the pontoon was enough of an answer for her to assume they were dead.

Or at least will be very soon.

She squared her jaw, fixing another arrow in place as the remaining Tarrazi closed in on them, thudding down the pontoon like a stampede. She hissed and cursed under her breath, assessing her options frantically.

We've been sent out here to an isolated position with no means of retreating to safer ground, she thought, her heart racing in her chest. *As soon as these invaders reach the harbour wall next to us, it'll be a knife-to-knife fight for survival.* She gulped, watching their blades glisten in black-gloved hands. *A knife-to-knife fight...*

And we brought the smaller knives.

With growing dread in the pit of her stomach, she aimed her arrow into the mass of bodies and looked for openings – managing a quick glance over to her comrade opposite, who—

Stared wide-eyed at the horizon, his face awash with fear; opening his mouth wide—

"Everybody down!"

She loosed her arrow blindly as the words left his mouth, dropping down onto her stomach as—

A whistling sound clipped the air over her head, passing between the archers like a shooting star—

Followed by a deafening *crack* of wood and metal, ringing out from somewhere behind her, showering her legs in dust and debris.

She looked back as the sound ruptured in her ears, flexing her toes like a cat ready to pounce. The storehouse there – a massive structure of wooden beams and metal panels – swayed unnaturally in the sea winds, as the nearest wooden pole buckled and trembled under a sudden increase in weight. The bottom portion of it had been blown off completely by the cannonball they had dodged, so that the entire south side of the building was held aloft only by thin metal sheets.

Studying it, she saw the rust at the edges of each panel, and the ancient bolts that rattled in their sockets, struggling to hold the structure in place. The entire cityscape beyond – up to the towering pinnacles of the palace keep in the distance – seemed to sway as the storehouse did, tilting the world on its axis.

That thing is gonna collapse any moment now, she deduced, pressing up on her hands. *We aren't safe here. We need to clear the area, and get out of here fast—*

The *sling* of a blade leaving its sheath tickled in her left ear, and all other concerns ceased to be suddenly as she shuddered like a lamb in a slaughterhouse.

Turning back to the other archers – prizing the knife from the small sheathe at her belt – she watched the few remaining Tarrazi saunter up the stone stairs onto the harbour wall next to them, their swords menacing with glee—

And then all hell broke loose in the blink of an eye.

She heard a scream, and saw one of her comrades topple with a gash down her front, carving her breast and collar open up to her fleshy neck.

A heartbeat later, and she saw the man who had been opposite her unsheathe his sword and block an attack, standing his ground against two of the enemy with little room to manoeuvre.

Behind, another archer hit the floor and pushed away with their hands, as an ugly brute lumbered towards them, reaching down to snag their hair and slit their throat.

The archer stood immediately at the sight of violence, flexing her knife, ready to engage with the invaders and save her comrades-in-arms—

When a massive coat of black armour blotted them all out like an eclipse, and a brutish figure appeared before her with a grin like glinting knives.

She bristled.

Oh shit—

"*Zoltha,*" they boomed, chuckling ominously. A huge, jagged blade pulled up close at their side; it looked almost comical in their massive hand. "*Dead-flesh.*"

"Come on then, you pale *freak,*" she spat, lowering down and flashing her teeth, dismissing all fear in her heart. "Come on then! Fucking fight me! *Come on!*"

Lifting their blade, the Tarrazi grinned, dragging their heel across the stone underfoot.

Before charging at her like a bull.

She stepped back, lurching away from the first strike as it cleaved down toward her head; bringing her knife up, she caught the second attack and skimmed along the blade's jagged edge as if she were back home tanning leather.

Another backstep, and she opened up space between them – lunging forward, she scratched the Tarrazi's breastplate superficially and cursed under her breath—

A forearm came down towards her head; she swung back and caught the cuff against her cheek. A numb knot of pain blanched her face, swelling with a bruise almost immediately.

The Tarrazi offered no respite and lunged back in with their blade, pushing up toward her exposed stomach—

She slid backwards and cut down, dragging her knife across the invader's knuckles with an ugly screech of steel, narrowly redirecting the attack aimed at her gut.

Seconds later, and their blades snapped together again, unwieldy and furious. A slice came in from the side, that she slapped away with a turn of the hips. Her own lunge nearly pierced their throat before the sword loomed and she retreated, defending another cleaving strike that would have taken her head from her shoulders.

An overhead attack came down, that she ducked with a twist of the knees. A left swing came through shortly after that, nearly cleaving her ribs apart like a steak joint. She diced and twisted with her tiny knife, shifting on her tiny feet, living on for just a few more moments between each perilous swing.

She held firm and held strong, and ground her teeth like a chisel, fighting against a Tarrazi as her forefathers had done for millennia before her. She was a tiny part of a battle that was eons long, perpetuating itself over and over with no sign of stopping or ceasing to be. Every attack that rained down on her, and every parrying strike she made in return, spoke of deep wounds that could never be healed, and deep pains that would never cease. A Tarrazi's pain of losing a war, and a homeland, and a way of life. A Provencian's pain of losing loved ones, and comrades, and it all ultimately being for nothing. Their pains were different, but their grief was shared, alongside their hate and their fury. Every swing of the blade carried with it centuries of toll, where one power had ruled over the other, and both had suffered because of it. There were no answers in the end: only blood and steel, and sorrow.

And a harbourside dashed with black and gold fire, as those same pains were exacted once more.

She curved her knife up against their chest-plate and stepped into the Tarrazi's circle, jamming a fist into their stomach-guard for good measure.

The Tarrazi wheezed above her, the balls of its eyes glinting furiously.

"That's for my mother, you *bastard*," she said, before stepping back and preparing for the next attack.

She manipulated the blade in her fingers, her mother's words recanting in her head as she moved from one form to the next. Her mother had been a diligent teacher for much of the archer's young life, drawing on her own training as a soldier to help her daughter grasp the ways of the bow. Although they had exchanged few stories from her time as a soldier, she knew that her mother had been an archer in the great war that had been fought fifty years prior: a massive conflict between the two peoples known historically as The Collapse. It had been a defining moment in the history of the Icebreaker Sea, so she had said: the battles that had been won set in motion everything that had happened since, from the Provenci Occupation to the civil war in the south.

And the attack on the harbour, too, manifesting before her in fire and smoke.

The Tarrazi brought their sword overhead and slit the sky in two; the young archer jolted away with a gasp as the blade slinged just past her breast. She attempted a lunge in retaliation – hoping to catch them off-guard – but was met with little reprieve as the Tarrazi bore down on her again.

All the same... all the fucking same, she growled, deflecting another attack. *So conniving and sinister, savouring every minute of it.*

Stabbing out with rage, she recounted the few stories her mother had told about the wars fought long ago, and the nature at which they'd been fought. Every one of them had carried the stench of horror, and her descriptions had elicited much the same: dead bodies dragged into piles to be burned; children with their throats carved out, strung up on trees like ornaments; looters scavenging armour and weapons, pawning them off to whichever scrouge would buy them. It was the foul nature of humanity, rearing its ugly head in the ashes of its own violence.

"*War is a curse, above all things,*" her mother had said on a cold day, returning home at the edge of a storm. "*It is a curse of people, and a curse of all that is good. We paint them as the enemy, and they shall paint us the same. But after what I've witnessed in war... and all the* horrors *those fucking Tarrazi caused my people... I want you to promise me one thing, my dear.*"

She remembered her mother's burning eyes, and the flash of pain in her heart, as she carved down against the Tarrazi, her enemy, with a rage building in her chest.

"*If war ever comes again, and the Tarrazi come at you in all their savagery, then make no hesitation, my dear...*"

The memory flashed—

The Tarrazi snarled—

Her mother's words echoed out in her ears—

"*...kill them* all.*"

The young archer screamed, wailing into the winds, and surged forward toward the towering Tarrazi with a raw fury burning over her cheeks.

The black-armoured figure cut across their body, hissing with frustration as they were suddenly on the defensive, using their brute strength to guide her away—

She slipped beneath the sword like a blade of grass in the wind, using the motions her mother had taught her so many years ago, stepping into their circle a heartbeat later—

To embed the blade in the soft of their neck, driving it up into their skull.

A crackle of spit emerged from the Tarrazi's gaping mouth, as a milkiness formed in the deep pits of their eyes. Their sword clattered to the ground with a painful chime of steel, their arms going limb and hollow. Their body hung above her for some moments, suspended at the end of her arm like a puppet, bringing fifty years of vitriol to a swift and gruesome end.

Swinging her arm to the side, she dragged the knife from the huge figure's neck and let them spill out over the cobbles next to her, oozing blood like a strange, gory fountain. As she lifted back onto shaky legs, the archer looked down on the massive corpse of the invader and curled her nose up in disgust.

That's for my dead mother… you pale fuckin' freak.

Ahead of her – in the dark and the gloom of the misty night – she found the fighting had stopped, and a few of her archers had survived to tell the tale. They stood staring blankly across the harbour, nursing wounds with butchered bodies at their feet, offering her little more than a smile as congratulations for her success. They appeared like ghosts to her, then, in the hollowness of the night: apparitions from her memory, imitating real life. Their skin was pale, almost like the bodies of the invaders at their feet. Every movement was slow and shaky, studying hands and swords with an awkward numbness that didn't really translate in their minds. What they had witnessed – and continued to witness in the wider harbour beyond – had changed them irreversibly, she knew, turning a corner from which they could never go back.

I've murdered people in cold blood, just to survive.

She looked to her own hands, coated in blood and dirt, and the sullied knife still clasped at her side. She felt the weight of them: the heaviness of her own grip against the world.

At least it's done now.

Looking back up to the other archers, she saw them gathering by the stone stairs, assessing their options with broad gestures and tired exhalations of breath. Some looked invigorated and ready for action, while others stared lifelessly at the waters below, lost in a trance of their own making. She couldn't hear their voices over the crashing waves to her left, only managing to pick out fragments of speech when the wind subsided for a moment.

After a while, one of the women among their half-dozen turned to her with a smile and a wave of the hand—

That quickly disappeared, as they looked past her with wide-eyes and made to scream—

With no noise coming out, as a silver bolt lanced through their windpipe and eviscerated them in an instant.

The woman blinked, and fell.

The other archers screamed.

The rise to violence dawned again, no sooner than it had finished.

The young archer stood fused to the spot, battling with a numbness she couldn't shift, wincing at the explosions of cannon-fire in the bay off to her left. Her mental dexterity ceased to be. Her spine rippled with unease. A horrifying tingle scattered at the base of her skull.

She turned slowly on her heel – slowly and fatefully – thinking of her mother's quiet songs and the feel of her soft hands, and looked north to the harbour beyond—

To watch a huge axe sail above her, dissecting the moon, aimed directly for her head.

IV

The Firestarter

The axe-blade connected with the woman's forehead like a knife through butter, prizing their skull open with an ungodly crack of bone, and a delighted grin curled across the big Tarrazi's face like a *skal* with their first practice sword.

Her entire face split open, slicing her brain in two. The axe carried through, such was its impossible strength, and embedded itself in her sternum, rupturing organs and vessels in a grotesque spout. Her perplexed, angered look of surprise fell away in an instant, as her legs crumpled and her blood spewed and she slid off the axe-blade like a dollop of warm custard.

Az-kabza, the Tarrazi mused, smirking at the gore.

Blood, or death.

Ahead of him, the sound of screaming echoed out over the harbourside: one of the other archers ran towards him, bellowing with tears in their eyes, likely at the death of their close comrade who now lay at his feet like a split log. They wielded a bloodied short-sword in one hand, dripping with blood, and sported a knife wound on their hip too. The anguish in their face was almost picturesque.

The big Tarrazi grunted at the disturbance, his face becoming stone.

Zoltha... never giving peace.

He hefted his axe, locking it in his gloved hands, and swung across his body – just as the archer stepped in and did likewise, whipping their sword toward his chest.

The archer's blade skimmed down the length of the Tarrazi's forearm, jarring against the metal plates there, bouncing off with no effect—

As his massive axe connected with the man's arm – with far greater reach than the archer's sword could ever manage – and severed it off at the shoulder.

The archer took on the colour of plaster, his eyes hollowing out. His mouth hung aghast, entirely speechless, staring dumbly at the stump that now constituted his left arm.

The Tarrazi opposite allowed himself a smirk, revelling in the shock of his victim, before he brought the axe across a second time without warning.

And carved the man's ribs open, killing him instantly.

The body hit the floor, and a howl went up from those around him. It was louder than the sea; louder than the cannons in the bay off to their right. His kin – his delighted brothers and sisters – revelled in his glory. They delighted in it. They danced in its blood.

Their time had come again.

"Az-kabza, my *feduzak!*" the huge Tarrazi bellowed, lifting his axe above his head and slapping his forearm like a drum. Around him, the other Tarrazi he had come ashore with did likewise, hefting their blades like glinting needles as gold and grey fire marked the horizon behind them. "Now, *go...*" The leader growled, pointing the end of his axe to the storehouses nearby. "Find *Zoltha...* burn *all!*"

The Tarrazi rallied around him, jeering and baying for blood, their armour like a great oil slick in the low, eerie light. They formed up shoulder-to-shoulder, closing in on all sides, before loping off down the narrow street ahead, spreading out across the harbourside in search of prey to gut. At the behest of their leader; at the whim of their gods in Their vaulted caves high above, bringing death wherever they came.

With a final glance back over the waves – marvelling at the huge ships as they jostled and tore at each other in the bay – the Tarrazi leader paced after his kin into the deeper recesses of the harbour, slipping under the shadow of a storehouse that seemed to inch closer to collapse with each gust of wind.

Away from the rasping sea and the distant, thunderous bellows of the cannons, a stillness came over the world around them, broken only by the clanking boots of the soldiers marching ahead into the dark. All the violence and destitution ceased; the sleepy tranquillity of night returned, albeit for a few moments. The huge figure took it in with a long draw of breath, taking a moment to place two fingers on his head and mutter a quiet prayer to the gods.

Find us, he proclaimed, gazing up at the clouds.

Thu... tü... tal.

He touched the fingers to his lips and tightened the grip on his axe, stepping out onto the wide street beyond which his kin had already crossed.

Thick stone slabs marked the ground beneath his feet, laid by the hands of Tarrazi workers over a millennia before, in a time long forgotten but never truly forgiven. Tiny rivers of sea-ooze lined the outskirts, dark with algae and the offal of harbour life. Metal-panelled storehouses rose up all around him, hunkered down like fat crabs with clutches of eggs beneath them. There were even a few tall citadels dotted between the storehouses, marked out against the city wall and the dim glow of the palace keep in the far distance.

Catching sight of the palace then – in all its vain futility – the Tarrazi curled his nose up with vehemence and spat on the stone at his feet. A sickness curled in his stomach: something like anger and something like pain, thinking on a great many sins and hating every one of them.

Foul place... dark place. Shadow place.

Memories came and went; stories and horrors all merged into one.

Burn...

All *need to burn.*

Turning back to the task at hand, he looked down the nearest side-street and spied movement there, as his soldiers paced down the alleyways like hunting dogs, sniffing the air for signs of the enemy that were no doubt lurking around. The air was ripe with their musk: their fear and their anger and their embarrassment. Caught with their tails between their legs, by a people who they thought they could rule over forever with no consequences. The air was full of it: arrogance, and shattered pride. The huge Tarrazi drew in long breaths, savouring the taste of it on his tongue.

Foolish Zoltha...

Never learn.

He took another step forward – pulling the grip tighter on his axe – and stopped suddenly, tensing his jaw. There were sounds somewhere off to his right, growing steadily louder: bellows and cries and clashing steel, reverberating off the storehouses' iron panels. They were sounds of violence, and madness in the dark.

Drawing steadily closer—

Turning right, he saw a number of his people emerge from behind one of the storehouses, forming up defensive lines across the street just ahead. A few of them had lost pieces of their armour; some held their thighs or forearms, applying pressure to fresh wounds. In the cold sea air, the big Tarrazi watched their heavy breaths rasp through their teeth like dragon's smoke.

Shortly after they appeared, a half-dozen well-armed *Zoltha* soldiers appeared from the same alleyway, adorned in steel cuirasses and chainmail leggings with vicious long-swords in their hands. They looked upon the Tarrazi with disgusted sneers, bashing their chests with their gloves, hurling ugly slurs at them like children.

And a heartbeat later, the *Zoltha* soldier charged at the Tarrazi line in a crush, screaming and hollering, hoping to breach their defences like a battering ram and tear them limb from limb—

But the Tarrazi launched from their positions before the *Zoltha* could reach them, swarming toward the enemy like bats hunting moths, dicing and cutting and snarling with a feverish desire for blood and ancient promises. They came together and wove together in one great mass of steel. From the leader's position further back, the street was lost in a haze of motion, as blades circled like fish-tails and the black armour glistened like oil. A seething, bloody mark against the harbourside.

Painted over and over again.

The big Tarrazi studied them for several moments – marvelling at their swordsmanship and guile – before turning away with a smirk and pacing across the street ahead. He knew that they needed no help from him, fending off the *Zoltha* that had appeared. With the power of the gods at their backs, and the great Queen's blessing from afar, the fate of the battle was all but sealed already. War was in the Tarrazi's very nature; it was an essence of their soul. Every battle was a blessing, gifted to those high above.

And there was no stopping their bloodshed, once the first drop had been spilt.

Feduzak fight… strong, the Tarrazi thought, slipping into the shadows of an alleyway with his echoey footsteps bouncing off the walls. *They will live… they will kill. The Zoltha will die.*

All must die…

He entered back out into the still moonlight moments later, with the sounds of fighting and cannon blasts little more than a faint echo at his back. A small cobbled square lay before him, surrounded by metal panel walls with rats scurrying along the gutters, squeaking and rustling loudly. The air was colder there, biting in his lungs, almost as if it were haunted. It was a forgotten place, after all: a tiny part of a massive city that many hardly realised was there. Tucked away in the bowels of the harbourside.

Hiding a sin that only the Tarrazi knew.

To his left, a squat building of stone blocks and wooden turrets stood out amongst the storehouses, appearing very dour and foreboding in the twilight. The torches had been snuffed out along its platformed roof, and its barred metal door had a faint orange glow behind it like the shutters on a furnace. To the untrained eye, it appeared just as unassuming as any other old building dotted along the harbourside of Casantri.

But for the Tarrazi leader – looking up at its ugly turrets and cracked stone walls – a deep despair welled in his chest at the sight of it, accompanied by an anger burning heavy in his chest, reciting stories his enemy had long forgotten.

Or choose to… ignore.

He approached the stone structure and looked over the metal door, picking out the sound of voices muttering in the room beyond. There was an edginess to the air around him: a tautness that he could almost pluck like a bowstring. It was palpable, and metallic-tasting on his lips, and stung his eyes like the sea winds.

He lifted his hand, placing it against one of the larger stones adjacent to the door, and ran his fingers over the crumbly surface. He felt his way across the rivets and grooves of the stone, like a baby sensing the world, until he reached the bottom right corner of the block where three long marks extended out in neat lines. The marks were a deep black – almost painful to the touch – and as he pulled his hand away there was a charcoal soot over his fingertips, pasting his skin like clay.

It was a quarry mark, he knew, etched into every stone block across the entire structure, from the salt-bleached floor to the rugged turrets at the top. It served as a reference point, indicating the region in Provenci's western mountains where the stone had first been mined many hundreds of generations before. The three prongs on the block before him acted as a sort of code about the stone's history, detailing an intricate past.

And the black plaster smudging them, indicated that the block had been put there by slaves.

Tarrazi slaves, the blackcoat leader acknowledged, rolling his tongue over his fang-like teeth. *My people, slaves… long ago.* He rubbed the black plaster between his fingers. *Zoltha raid villages… stealing people, taking away… made work until they bleed. Until they die.*

He recounted a memory, bitter in his heart, of his father from long ago: how he had escaped the camps up in the mountains after several long years as a slave, and found his way home stowed away on a mule-cart. The big Tarrazi remembered the elation he had felt, after finally seeing his father again; the whole village had sung and rejoiced and prayed for many nights, thanking the gods for Their mercy and his safe return.

But his father had become something different after the years trapped in the camps: something distant and *other,* that could not be explained. A darkness fell upon him that nothing could shift. He never spoke; he rarely ate; his skin lay gaunt around his face, with deep eyes that saw everything and nothing all at once. He recounted nothing of his time as a slave worker; he had no stories of the quarry, or his *Zoltha* masters. He was a ghost: a hollowed out shell of the man from before.

They had taken it all from him, in the end.

And it was little more than two months after his initial return that he succumbed to an unknown disease, and was snuffed from the world like the snap of a crossbow, never hitting its intended target.

He died... no answers, the Tarrazi leader thought, thinking back to his father's funeral pyre and the man's sad, resolute eyes. *Never answers... only enemies. Those to blame. Those who hurt him.*

An anger seethed within him suddenly, dispatching all other emotion.

Zoltha did it. Zoltha kill him. Zoltha took... from me.

He snarled, stepping in front of the barred metal door, flashing his teeth like a wolf.

They... they all... must...

Die.

He lurched forward, kicking out with a steel-cap boot, and blasted the door open, breaking the silence with a snap of locks and a bellow of indiscriminate rage.

The door clattered against the interior wall with a sound like ricocheting bolts, exposing the room beyond to the rasping winds of night.

The orange glow of candles coated every surface, like blooms of algae across the stone walls and wooden doors. Small round tables and ugly squat stools dotted the outskirts of the thin corridor ahead, where at least ten fully-armoured *Zoltha* sat shuffling cards and rolling dice. They were joking and laughing with each other in hushed voices, gesturing openly and slapping their backs, completely ignorant of the destruction going on just outside. As if it wasn't their problem and the Tarrazi weren't there enemy.

How wrong… they are.

At the abrupt sound of crashing metal, the soldiers turned to attention—

And rose from their stools with a scrape of stone, their eyes bulging wildly at the huge figure now occupying the doorway beyond.

Hands reached for blades on instinct; a silence descended, assessing motives and next moves. The candlelight seemed to dim as the Tarrazi took a single step forward, looking between each frightened face with a persecuting smile.

"What d'you want… freak!" one of the *Zoltha* shouted, thrusting their sword out defiantly. "We want no trouble, so just… get out 'n' go the fuck back where you came from, yea? We ain't botherin' you, so don't go botherin' us."

The Tarrazi said nothing in response; he looked to his feet for a moment, and slipped something from his waistband.

"Did you fuckin' hear me or not, then, you *freak?*" the soldier shouted again, less confident this time. The other soldiers bristled around him. "I don't know if you're understanding me, but I *said* can you—"

"No," the Tarrazi replied, squaring his jaw and staring deep into the man's soul, watching them visibly shrink away under his harrowing gaze. "Because… this, not over… it only just… *start.*"

Without a word more, the huge Tarrazi lifted the item from his waistband up into the light, displaying it in his outstretched palm for all to see.

It was a tiny vial of black liquid, sloshing delicately behind the glass in rolling waves. Against the candlelight, it was almost luminescent, displaying a myriad of colours across the interior rim. It looked so insignificant, on the surface of the Tarrazi's pale hand. So small and unruly.

But, at the sight of it, the soldiers down the corridor visibly recoiled, steadying themselves against the walls as a shock rippled between them, realising what it was.

Oil.

"All *Zoltha...* must die," the Tarrazi growled, curling his huge fingers around the vial. He looked between each of his victims one at a time, measuring them up, before his gaze fixed on the corridor's back wall.

"All *Zoltha...* will *BURN!*"

The Tarrazi pulled back and launched the vial over the soldiers' heads, watching it sail across the room like a cannonball in the low light—

It shattered against a table at the back of the room, spilling over a cluster of candles that flickered delicately—

Igniting the oil: setting the liquid aflame as it spilled over the table edge and arced toward the back wall—

Where it splattered over a pair of powder barrels wedged in the corner, producing a terrifying *hiss.*

The guards heard the noise and gasped, sweat spilling down their foreheads in tiny rivers.

They looked ahead again – to the cold, open air of the harbour-side beyond – and watched the huge Tarrazi step back with his hand fixed to the door handle, a sadistic grin laced over his face that twinkled at the ends of his fangs.

Zoltha... burn.

Recognising their fate, the soldiers screamed suddenly and lurched forwards in a crush—

Opposite them, the Tarrazi stepped back and slammed the door shut with a tremendous crack of steel. Jarring his wrist suddenly, he bellowed and broke the door handle in a shower of metal parts, as an intense burning smell pulled through his nostrils and stung his pearlescent black eyes.

Screeches echoed from within the stone barracks. Cries of fear tapped through his ears. The glow around the doorframe became impossibly bright—

The Tarrazi took several steps back, smiling sadistically, studying the marks on the blocks one more time as they glowed and vibrated with an ancient vengeance. He took a deep, steady breath, taking in the smoky night air—

Before an explosion rocked the harbourside around him, and his vision was consumed in deadly fire.

The entire south side of the barracks tore apart in a balloon of orange and gold, throwing stone and debris out over the surrounding buildings. Jets of smoke roared skyward, as the powder crackled and hissed and detonated over and over again, coating the skies in light and sparks. Flame consumed all things, drowning out the screams of the soldiers and the snapping of wood beams and the unadulterated chaos that claimed the world before him.

The Tarrazi looked upon it all with a glow of delight: witnessing a destruction of his own making, exacting the will of his people on their most ancient enemy. It was a reprisal of a sin committed centuries before, buried for centuries past. It was a mercy to his father, and the slaves, and every other Tarrazi soul brought under the heel of the regime.

Stood in the cobbled square, he opened his arms out and bellowed. He laughed and cried. He screamed.

The heat swept across his skin; his tears evaporated on his cheeks, running over the creases of his smiling, grieving face. He opened his palms to the sky, offering the sacrifice out to the gods, praying for death and beauty under the crackles of powder fire.

The moonlight glistened through the clouds above. Flashes of light danced over the horizon all around.

A warmth overcame him: a wonderous heat, pulling over his arms and his chest. It rippled down his legs; it shivered over his pale scalp.

Twisting down his neck—

Down the right side of his neck, in particular—

A warmth and intensity, verging on... *pain*—

Actual pain, snapping down his collarbone and into his lungs—

He stuttered, and found he could hardly breathe; a cough escaped his lips—

There was iron on his tongue, coating his gums. Something was spilling down his chin—

He reached up to his neck, clawing at air as his limbs seemed to stop working, trying to ascertain what the pain was—

Feeling a handle there by his ears, and a hilt, and the sharp base of a small knife-blade—

Embedded in his throat.

How...

He hadn't even felt it happen. He didn't even register that he had been wounded.

It made no sense—

His skin crawled and his stomach lurched; he stood baffled at the flames, trying to make sense of it. Orange flashed in his eyes; welts of blood spurted down his neck.

Slowly, numbly, the Tarrazi turned to his right, blinking into the dark from where the knife had come from—

To spy there an old man with a shaved head, adorned in grey Provencian robes, their face awash with horror and confusion.

The Tarrazi had no idea who the man was, or how long they had been there. He had no idea how they had managed to stick a knife in his neck, at that. His skin crawled as if it were covered in lice, staring at the man who stared at him with a look of horror usually saved for the dying or dead.

The Tarrazi reached for the knife in his neck again, but found he couldn't even lift his arms. He attempted a step forward, only for his knee to buckle awkwardly and refuse to budge.

The man opposite did nothing in response, regarding him blankly. They couldn't believe what they had done – perhaps they hadn't even *meant* to kill him.

Lost in disbelief, with a warmth flooding his body, the huge Tarrazi took a stumbling step forward and reached out toward the *Zoltha,* a cry on the end of his tongue.

"What… have you *done*—"

V

The Citizen

The strange man keeled over in front of him, frothing blood at the mouth, and collapsed onto the cobbles in a dead, crumpled heap. The sound of his armour slapping against the stone made the old man jump, and he only just placed his hands over his face in time to suppress a scream.

He didn't even know who the man was – or rather, who they had been before their untimely demise. The old man had heard an explosion, and then screaming, and as he had turned the corner to see what was going on, he spied the pale figure with their hands in the air, babbling about some god or other in a language he could hardly understand. It was a hellish scene, like something he had seen in the Old Texts when he was just a boy. He saw the burning barracks and the thick plumes of powder smoke; he heard the strangled cries of the soldiers trapped in the fiery maw. And this person – this figure, whoever they were – was revelling in it like some demon, crying and laughing all in one.

A wave of panic had overcome the old man in that moment, consuming any rationality he possessed. He wanted to try and save those trapped in the blaze; he wanted to have revenge against the perpetrator stood before him. His skin crawled and his gut lurched, and in the end he acted with a primal instinct he hadn't even realised he possessed.

Raising his trusty knife, hidden away in the folds of his robe for protection, he speared it down over the rim of the man's black chest-plate, and lodged it in their neck.

And at first, when no response came, some dull part of him thought he had missed. Despite the blood spurting from the wound in a fountain, and the blood that lay smeared across his palms, the lack of response from the huge man made him wonder if he had somehow imagined it, and it was all some strange, twisted dream. That the barracks weren't really on fire; that the soldiers inside weren't really dead.

And then the pale figure's face had creased up – presenting the kind of ugly expression one gives before sneezing – and any doubt the old man had about what he had done dissolved in an instant.

"And now… I stand here… with a *dead man*… at my…" he rasped, looking down at the pale corpse and the blood forming rivers between the cobbles. A bubble of sick popped in his throat. "Oh… *gods*…"

Next to him, another small explosion sent a jet of fire skyward that fizzed and spat with ignition powder. The old man shied away from it, blinking dumbly at the maw of flame, and only one thought surfaced in his mind long enough to make any sense.

I have to get away from here.

I have to get away…

He turned on his heel, stumbling away from the cobbled square like a colt with the wind up its tail, skittering off into the dark with no idea where he should go, or where was even safe. The moonlight offered no answers; the shadows only sought to swallow him whole. The echoing chimes of steel and screams were relentless in his ears, coming from every angle all at once.

He turned down an alleyway and traipsed slowly forward, startled by a sudden splashing to his left as rats bolted for the nearest sewer. The smell of sewage and sea-salt accompanied him as he walked: smells that coiled up in his nostrils like worms and stung his eyes with their intensity. Cold prickles ran up his back like needles, too, as his fingers felt over the walls on either side and kept him steady, moving slowly forward through the gloom with a beam of solid moonlight in the distance.

What am I doing here? he thought for a moment, uncertain about whether he should laugh or cry at the question. *It's the middle of the night. Who are all of these people… and the noises… is, is that cannon-fire? Why's everyone shouting so much?*

What's even going on?

He found the answers were unforthcoming, and his mind wandered elsewhere. In a tired malaise, he almost considered going back to his office a few streets away and curling back up on his armchair for the night, forgetting the whole affair had even happened at all—

When a ripple of voices caught in his ears from somewhere ahead, and the orange glow of torches grew steadily brighter there.

His eyes widened.

The air caught in his throat—

He pressed up against the nearest wall – cursing under his breath at the *clang* of the iron panels – and placed his palms flat against the metal, absorbed for a moment by the wonderful coolness against his fingertips.

At the opposite end of the alleyway, the orange glow of torches continued to grow and grow, and the drumming clatter of steel boots sent his heart knocking against his ribs. Seconds passed by; heart-beats, even, as the marching grew louder and the street grew even brighter—

Figures crossed the end of the alleyway suddenly, under the amber glow of torches. There were at least ten of them in total – and none of them were Provencian, he realised. They were large and dark and imposing; they had pale faces like woven cloth affixed with salivating snarls. The glint of steel hung in their hands, menacing and deadly.

They seemed to just pass the alleyway by at first, pressing on with great intent to some unknown target beyond, jabbering between each other in the same indecipherable language he had heard from the other man at the barracks—

Then a torch flashed across the front of the alleyway, illuminating it like a port-hole, held aloft in the clawed hands of a creature most foul.

It had porcelain skin and pointed teeth. It had black marks along the top of its right cheek, hardly visible in the light. Its eyes were like black orbs, with black veins snaking up its neck. A single braid of wiry hair traced down the middle of its earless scalp. There was a look of hunger behind its gaze, too, lusting for blood. It was a look of malice, if he had ever seen one.

A look of hate, too....

He had never seen anything like it. He didn't think even think something like it could exist. It betrayed all notion of reality in his mind.

What the hell even is that thing?

It stood for a moment – peering deep into the darkness of the alleyway beyond, picking apart the shadows – and for a moment he thought he would be discovered. But, after a few heartbeats, the creature turned with a dismissive grunt and loped off after its kin, leaving the old man alone in the alleyway once more, breathless and entirely afraid.

What was...

What was that...

He lifted his hands to his face and rubbed his eyes, hoping to dispel the image and banish the nightmare altogether. He pushed against his sockets with his palms; he clawed at his skin like a feral beast. But even then, when his eyes snapped open, all he could see was the face of the pale creature and the smeary blood on his hands, coating his skin with stains that he knew would never wash out.

There was blood.

Blood everywhere.

Dark shadows.

Pale faces and black eyes—

"Oh gods... oh gods, someone *help me...*" he whimpered, stumbling toward another alleyway that intersected the one he was on. Tears pulled over his cheeks as he swayed from wall to wall absently, hardly able to keep himself upright. A weight coiled itself around his neck, refusing to let go. The clouds above looked like they were plummeting.

"*Someone help me please...*"

Stumbling forward, he clattered against an iron panel and shuddered at the sound, hardly aware of his own body in that moment, lost in the depths of his fear.

The image of the face reappeared one moment, slipping away the next like a gust of wind—

Clattering boots marched past him, only for him to find there was nothing there—

He flinched, jumping at shadows—

Nothing appeared, despite the noise in his head, rolling over and over again—

Snapping.

Snarling.

Slashing steel—

"Someone... anyone... *help*..."

He lurched into an alcove of an old stone building and slumped down on the first step, shivering with fear and cold and pain and exhaustion. Tears rolled down his cheeks, red-raw around his eyes. Nausea claimed him in waves; he retched sporadically with nothing to show for it.

In the darkness of night, he was so very alone.

Why has this happened? he pleaded to himself, looking up to the shrivelled clouds. *I... I've been here all my life... done this all my life, with no problem. Through wars and blockades and... and... I've just run this quarter, doing my business, filing my papers and stamping... I've, I've been stamping...*

What are they? He breathed deeply, with a tremble. *Why are they here? Are they... are they here to kill us? To hurt us—*

Oh, gods, am I gonna die? Am I gonna die here?

I can't die here! I can't die in this place, to those things—

I've... I've been here all my life... they can't...

They can't…

Oh, gods…

He looked up into the spiralling skies high above and saw the moon emerge briefly from behind the clouds, showering the world in pale rays before slipping from sight once again.

As the darkness returned, he managed a sob of fear, with a weight pressing heavy on his soul.

"Just *kill me*," he whispered out into the nothing, so desperate and so very alone.

"Just… kill *me*—"

From somewhere in the alcove behind him, a rasp of breath pulled up his neck.

"*With pleasure,*" a voice said—

As a knife-blade slit his throat.

VI

The Shadow

She stepped out from the shadows of the alcove with blood dripping down her blade and inhaled deeply. The air was salty and cool, stinging in her lungs like nettles. The acrid bitterness of smoke lingered on her tongue. It was nostalgic, almost, of a time long past and a version of her that she had long forgotten. Of crescent waves and billowing winds and the creak of a ship-mast overhead. Covering the known world on the deck of a beautiful vessel, chasing the horizon under the stars. They had been merciful years, she knew, where things had been easier and life had seemed so full. Where the world and the sea were so vast and limitless.

And death wasn't always at her back, trying to break down her door.

She sighed, dismissing the thought out of hand, and looked down to the cobbles at her feet, where the body of the old man lay twisted and still, blood leaking from their neck in a long stream. He had been hysterical when he first appeared: taking air into his lungs in frightful sobs, as his entire world came crashing down and cold reality rose to meet it. He cried like a man who had never known fear before; he cried like a baby in a thunderstorm, longing for his *marzedna's* comforting embrace. And when he had collapsed on the step before her in a pile of frail old limbs, a tiny knot of empathy had twisted in her chest, hearing those weeping cries. Something quiet and sorrowful. Of memories long past; of feelings long forgotten. All of it compounding into one, rolling over again and again – before it was snuffed out by the draw of her knife and the sickly snarl on her face, as she buried her past and drew upon her anger.

And slit his throat like a feckless pig.

Looking down upon his body then, and the silver rounds of his bloodshot eyes, she curled her nose up and wiped her knife on the ugly folds of his robe. All empathy she held, was buried deep and wiped clean. There was no time for mercy or pity.

Only the cruellest survive.

She stepped past the corpse and looked up and down the street, sliding her knife into its sheath as she did so. Stooping low, she darted off to the right and slipped down the nearest alleyway, her black cowl billowing in the sea breeze as her feet padded silently against the stone. The dripping gutters tapped delicately in her ears; scurrying rats shot down into the drains, squeaking furiously at her disruption. Mildew clung to the walls around her like rotten fruit, flashing with a strange phosphorescence as she swept past with the wind pulling up at her back.

Reaching the end of the alleyway, she approached a wider street and stopped abruptly, peering out from her concealed vantage point on the wider world beyond. There were signs of a struggle there, she acknowledged: the stone slabs ahead were covered in smears and dirty marks, with the imprints of boots scraping the ground in random places. Tiny shards of broken armour dotted the stones like fish-scales, alongside the occasional discarded blade or loose coil of chainmail.

Soldiers fought here recently, she mused, biting at her lip, *pitted against each other with sharpened blades and vengeful smiles. Quite a big fight by the looks of it... and no way of knowing who won—*

Or so she thought, that waa, until she saw the pile of Provencian corpses wedged against a house to her left, swarmed by a million flies.

There were at least a dozen of them, by her best estimate, with rivers of blood dripping down their faces and swelling in the pits of their eyes. Their mouths hung agape, frozen with shock, staring blindly up at the moon in wonder.

Looking upon them, she grunted with disgust and pulled a gaiter over her nose, catching the faintest scent of flesh as the wind fell away for a moment. She found the butchery to be quite distasteful, and placed a hand against her stomach to quash the nausea growing there. In her bountiful experience, killing was an art form best exercised with swiftness and grace, exacting a toll upon one's enemies without any excess. But when that art was compounded with the violence of war, the swiftness and grace she exulted in was entirely lost, and was replaced instead with an ugly word that smelled even worse than the pile of corpses.

Results.

A sourness folded over her tongue as the word flashed behind her eyes.

So brutal… and so unnecessary.

Pressing her palm against the nearest wall, she turned away and crossed the main street like a fox, passing under the moon's watchful eye for a matter of heartbeats before slipping into the shadows once more.

Shooting down the next alleyway with the squawk of crows at her back, she stopped at the far end and looked out on a rank of massive storehouses, spreading left-to-right as far as she could see. Their ugly metal panels were rusting at the edges, and were coated in a slick grey slime that seemed to collect in the gutters like tar. It looked like any other rank of storehouses, in any other place along the harbourside – but even so, she recognised where she was almost immediately, mapping the harbourside out in her mind with an intricate, neurotic detail.

There are five storehouses here, with a small military barracks at the end by the city wall, manned by ten regular guards. Another rank of three storehouses mark the next street over, dissected by three small cobbled squares that are frequented by stowaway drunks. After that, we find the merchant offices looking out on the main thoroughfare, stretching from the sea to the city wall with small alleyways in-between. She smiled, rolling her fingers together. *And that means that, from here, there are only two streets left until my destination is in sight...*

The knife at her side grew warmer against her thigh.

Her smile turned to a grin.

How... efficient.

She turned right and skulked along the storehouse walls like a phantom, retracing paths she had memorised over the previous few days while living in the shadows of the enemy. Her part in the Tarrazi's grand plan – much like her art of killing – relied on her knowledge of stealth and deceit, and she had been sought out by her superiors specifically because of it. Sent on a long boat down the coast, she had landed on the shoreline just north of the harbour and snuck past the guards manning the walls, slipping into the beating heart of the enemy without so much as a whisper.

From there, she had found an abandoned attic space in one of the houses on the waterfront, using it as a base of operations as she traipsed the narrow streets of the harbour, noting the number of guards present at night and where their barracks were, and how easy it was to get from place to place. She was diligent in her research, and methodical in her work. She needed no map nor reference point to determine what she found: every street corner and alley opening affixed a place in her mind that she could recall whenever she wished, until the entire harbourside looked no different than the back of her hand.

Familiar, and yet not even slightly her own.

She slipped between two storehouses with a splash of surface water, continuing on her path west through the labyrinth of buildings with a dogged determination only her people possessed.

Ahead of her, over the lip of another stone structure, she spied the upper reaches of the city walls spearing out into the night, dotted with flickering orange torches. There were no soldiers manning the turrets, she noted, as she scanned the upper reaches for silver domed helmets and found nothing but clear air and firelight. They were most likely engaged elsewhere, she knew, pressing south toward the shipbuilding quarter to protect their precious supplies.

And for me, in the far north keeping to the shadows... well, that sounds just grand.

She entered out onto a narrow street and turned down the next alleyway to her right, narrowing her shoulders like a ship-mast to avoid scraping against either wall. In the narrow confines, a claustrophobia pulled at her heart for a few moments, peering up at the gutters above her, imagining them teetering over and burying her beneath, with no way to escape and no hope of survival—

She sucked in a quick breath and stepped out of the alleyway, entering out into one of the small squares that lay bathed in radiant moonlight—

Where two soldiers looked up at her with a sudden, profound shock, their hands dropping almost immediately to the blades at their sides.

What the—

She ground to a stop and opened her hands out beside her, caught in their line of sight with nowhere left to hide. Prickles of sweat pulled up her nape in a heartbeat; her breath felt hot and ragged through her lips. A cloud shifted overhead, coating the square in a dour greyness.

Time slowed.

The leftmost guard lifted his hand.

"Where do you—"

She flicked a tiny blade from the cuff of her sleeve, throwing it at the leftmost soldier with a delicate twist of her fingers—

As it impaled his throat, opening his windpipe with a warm gush of blood that seemed to appear from nowhere—

He clawed at his neck with bulging eyes, inhaling blood as if he were drowning. A paleness coated his skin, sucking the life from his body as his knees gave in, toppling him like an aggrieved toddler at the cusp of an agitated wail.

The soldier next to him gasped and drew his blade; the Tarrazi did likewise, whipping the knife into her hand with a cool certainty that betrayed the panic streaming through her body.

She lunged forward on instinct, crossing the distance between them with an effortless grace—

The soldier gawked at her dumbly and opened his mouth, the machinations of a scream forming on his tongue—

She struck out with the knife—

A noise escaped his lips—

That was immediately deadened by the blade driven up through his neck, piercing his oesophagus like a skewer.

Staring deep into his eyes as the light there dimmed, she released a breath through pursed lips and wore a face of stone. There was no room for grief or guilt when exacting a silent death. Their demise was a tiny, unfortunate part in the greater plan: a plan that she had no part in devising, but was entirely devoted to exacting. Their deaths were therefore meaningless, and without consequence.

For death is always knocking...

She withdrew the knife and let the body slump to the floor, joining his comrade in the next life as he too succumbed to his wounds.

...and now is not my time.

Wiping her blade on the soldier's cloth undershirt, she slid it back into its sheath with an effortless silence and listened out to the whispers of the wind. Beneath the whistles and eddies of the constant sea breeze – and the faded *boom* of cannons somewhere to the far east – she heard the sound of marching boots and the rallying cries of soldiers in the distance, a few streets away at her back. Whether they had been alerted to the soldier's cry before she had run him through, or were just doing a sweep of the area in search of Tarrazi invaders, she wasn't sure: all she did know was lingering around the corpses of one's enemy was a bad omen in of itself, and the sooner she fled the scene, the better.

Stepping over the pools of blood now staining the cobbles below, she swept down the alleyway on her left and disappeared back into the shadows, meandering between the squat buildings like a hunting dog. The altercation had cost her valuable time, and she knew that the other players in the master plan would be at their destination soon enough. The part she played in everything relied on her swiftness and guile.

And she had no intention of letting them down, when she was so close to the end.

She twisted on her heel and made a sharp right, before skirting left again just as fast. She moved with a frightful momentum, her footsteps near-silent in the din. The buildings narrowed around her as she streamed forward, shrinking down to single-storeys as she made a final turn, darting along a narrow path with merchant signs swinging overhead, and the sprawling, moonlit expanse of a wide street in the space just beyond.

Digging her heels in, she pressed up against the edge of the merchant's house and released another breath. Taking some time to steady herself, she peered around the corner toward the city walls and the sprawling metropolis it encased.

To find her destination laid out before her, spanning across the end of the street, marking the end of her journey and the finale of her work.

The gatehouse was a monolith looking out on the northern harbour, squat between two massive turrets of stone with a walkway across its upper edge. The gate itself was wide and heavy-set, designed for pedestrian access with just enough room for horses and carts. In the low light, the metal bars looked almost like teeth, and the numerous guards dotting the walkway above looked like pieces on a game-board, guided by an unseen hand.

From the street below, she looked over the gatehouse in sections, assessing for anything that she may have missed during her previous encounters. There were more guards present than normal, she noted, as well as more torches along the walkway above, but with the attack raging in the bay somewhere at her back, it came as no real surprise. Craning her neck slightly further, the two towers to either side also seemed unchanged, and the gate itself lay firmly shut as expected. But the small pedestrian gate on the far right-hand side was also sealed shut for some reason, and had been manned by four heavily armed guards with no intention of letting anyone through.

She frowned, furrowing her brow over her black eyes. *Unusual,* she thought. *There are no reinforcements coming... the soldiers in the barracks out here are all alone. Perhaps those in power underestimate our strength and numbers...*

...or perhaps those on the harbour aren't worth their effort.

Logging the analysis in her mind, she turned away from the gatehouse and retreated back down the alleyway, heading down a different path west towards the main city from there.

Approaching the far end, she gazed up at the huge stone walls looming above her, with torches lining its upper edge ominously. The gatehouse tower was now on her right, it's turrets jutting up like rotten teeth against the moon, appearing somehow even larger from that angle than before.

But she paid the magnitude of everything little attention, having walked past the same walls several times over the previous days. It was a pointless observation to make for the task at hand, and only sought to churn her anxiety in her chest if she thought of it for too long. Instead, she turned her interest to the outer wall of the nearest tower.

And the tiny opening there manned by a single guard, leading to a staircase into the gatehouse itself.

One access point; one flight of stairs. The stairs open out onto a platform within the tower, adjacent to the main walkway over the gate. The main lever is located somewhere along that walkway, likely protected by a horde of Zoltha soldiers.

She gritted her teeth and sighed.

This will be... less than efficient.

Reaching down to her side, she pulled an old square of cloth from a hook on her belt, followed by a thin vial of a deep green, slightly gaseous liquid. Adjusting them both in her hands, she pried the vial open gently and splashed it against the cloth with three short swipes, before sealing the lid again and throwing it down at her feet.

Holding the cloth down by her thigh, the liquid's pungent odour crawled into her nostrils almost immediately, diffusing through her senses like a parasitic worm. She pressed a hand over her mouth to stop any coughing or wheezing, as the potency took hold and convulsions rocked her stomach. Even the faintest smell of it brought a haziness in her eyes, which she only just managed to fight off.

Madra root, she thought, squeezing her nose beneath the gaiter. *The most potent sedative in the known world...*

And it stinks like piss.

Taking in deep breaths of cool sea air, she looked around the corner of the merchant's house and watched the guard at the tower turn away from her for a moment, facing toward the gatehouse and the wide street beyond. She could pick out the sound of whistling over the quiet rasp of the wind, as the guard looked down to their hands and adjusted their leather gloves.

Wasting no time, she kicked out on the balls of her feet and bolted across the narrow road, closing the distance in a matter of seconds with her pulse pounding through her skull.

Reaching the guard – who started turning back as she approached – she swung her arm up around their neck and pressed the cloth into their nose, smothering their mouth as they attempted a scream—

With no noise emerging, as the *madra* root did its devilish work and they slid to the floor in silence, passing into the unconscious void without so much as a whisper.

Not even a heartbeat had passed.

Just perfect.

The Tarrazi released her breath and eased the cloth from the guard's mouth, throwing it into the gutter and wiping her hand clean.

Checking around the corner to see if anyone had spotted her from the gatehouse, she hoisted the soldier's unconscious body and dragged them into the tower with her, slipping back into the delicate shadows where she knew she always belonged.

Once inside – bathed in the dim glow of torchlight – she pulled the body beneath a winding wooden staircase and deposited them unceremoniously behind some boxes, letting their arms fold in on themselves almost in prayer. The soldier looked almost blissful in the ambivalent light.

May sleep guide your soul, the Tarrazi whispered within.

And may you never wake up again…

She stepped back and took a moment to orientate herself, moving against the nearest wall and peering up into the dizzying heights of the tower above. It was lit by sconces throughout, and the spiral wooden stairway circled the structure consistently all the way to a platform at the top. By the lack of noise emanating from the space above, she also safely assumed that there were no guards present, allowing her to crawl up the neck of the enemy without anyone noticing.

Drawing her knife premeditatedly, she pressed her leather sole down on the first step and delighted at the lack of noise it made under her weight. Despite the apparent age of the wood, and the depressions in the panel from decades of use, it appeared just as sturdy as any other. She knew it would be foolish to assume the entire stairway would be as quiet, it was true, but with the first step as a positive marker for what came next, she made no hesitation in launching up the first flight and turning to the next just as fast.

After a while, she was clearing entire storeys with great sweeping lunges, gliding up each stairway as if she were at one with the wind. She hardly broke her stride with each turn; she hardly lost her breath, ascending the tower with a focused energy and an unswaying mind. The constant motion embodied her, moving with her like a fish upstream, channelling through the rapids until she reached the very top of the stairway, and peered delicately over the lip of the platform to observe what lay beyond.

An opening stood opposite her, leading out onto the long walkway that bridged the gatehouse to the next tower. She counted roughly ten soldiers dotted along the parapets, each of them illuminated by orange flame. They all stood to the right-hand side facing east, looking out towards the bay in the distance where the ships were still locked in perilous battle. They paid little attention to anything else going on around them, oblivious to the world – to the point where a crow hopped along the battlements at their backs, squawking loudly, and no one so much as looked over their shoulder.

Lifting up from the platform gently – becoming suddenly aware of the sound of voices in a closed room to her left – she paced slowly over to the tower's inner wall and kept her eyes locked on the walkway ahead. She knew this was the riskiest part of her mission, and the part that everything else was counting on. She had been told as much during her brief reconnaissance before setting off on the longboat south, alongside the rather foreboding missive of *'you may not return in one piece'*.

But I do not fear death when it comes knocking: we are one and the same, in the end, she mused, as her gaze passed from face to face down the walkway ahead. *I exact death on others, and death always watches me. One day I will live; the next, I will not. It can be taken away like the strike of a match...*

She looked to the stone floor ahead of her and smiled.

...or the crank of an iron lever.

Down the small flight of steps between the tower door and the walkway, a large iron gear had been set into the floor with a number of mechanisms surrounding it – including a long metal rod with a cloth handle, fixed into position like a windswept tree. It stood in the moonlight gleaning, almost enticing her to it: the final part and the end of her journey, only a few meagre steps away.

But even now, so close to my success... there remains one small catch, she acknowledged, as her eyes crossed to a pair of boots stood alongside the lever.

And the huge armoured sentinel who wore them, positioned against the outer wall like a gargoyle.

They were an imposing figure against the harshness of the moon, with an impressive steel spear gripped in their padded gloves, reflecting the watchful force behind their eyes. They straddled the lever possessively, clearly aware of its importance, and how if the lever fell and the gates fell open, all hell would break loose.

Which was exactly the mission that the Tarrazi had been assigned, and why she was even there in the first place – much to her now-evident disgust, denting her perfect plan.

Bastards, she hissed, running through a thousand options about what to do next. *Perhaps I can open the gates and break the lever before they have a chance to respond... then I can run back here and descend the stairway, hoping I don't get shot on the way down.*

She looked to the top of staircase, and then back to the walkway ahead, noting each soldier in turn and their obvious lack of awareness.

They're oblivious... so sucked in by the battle in the bay that they wouldn't even notice me... couldn't notice me, if I just slipped past and activated the lever...

She peered down at the knife in her hand, then up to the moon blanching the clouds high above.

This must be it, then, came her final thought, fearless and burdened with steel. *Time to face death at the door.*

Time to answer death knocking.

Whispering a prayer, she bent low to the ground like a vulture and skittered silently over to the lever, passing beneath the sentinel's shadow. She could feel the heat coming off their body; she could hear their ragged breath inhaling deeply. The Tarrazi's heart seemed to press up against her ribs, stifling her breath.

Slowly, delicately, she placed her fingers around the cloth handle of the lever, and used her other hand to place the knife-blade down into the base of the gears—

Gently—

Gently—

As the sentinel turned suddenly and looked down at her, deadly fires burning in their eyes with shock and horror and fury—

The Tarrazi snarled with fear and cranked the lever down, jamming her knife into the gears and breaking the mechanism as a shout went up from the sentinel and the other soldiers turned towards them—

The Tarrazi launched up from her position, catching sight of a spear-tip lowering towards her—

Turning back to the tower, and the opening that marked her narrow escape route—

Where two Provencian soldiers now stood, reaching for their blades with venom on their tongues—

As she stopped, and stalled, and muttered a fatal curse under her breath...

... as a spear lanced up through her stomach, protruding from her sternum like a needle through fabric.

Darkness swept in almost immediately; the spear point glinted beneath her.

She studied it...

There was blood on her tongue; in her throat...

There was tiredness...

Silence; numbness...

Blinking...

Blinking...

Blinking...

...death, knocking...

VII

The Gatekeeper

The sentinel pulled the spear from the intruder's body and pressed a hand between their shoulder-blades, shoving them to the ground and pinning a knee against their back. As she did so, blood flushed from the wound in the figure's stomach, drenching the stone below in a grim pool of human essence. There was no resistance from the body beneath her. There was no attempt at escape. The spear-wound had killed them outright.

But their presence was a more terrifying prospect than their death ever could be.

"Search the tower, *now!*" the sentinel howled, gritting her teeth. "See if there are any more. *Go!*"

The two guards at the door of the tower scampered away at her bellows, pulling helmets down over their faces and adjusting the swords in their hands. They moved in panicked stutters, grappling for control—

"Ma'am?"

The voice same from her left; the sentinel turned to find one of the other guards looming next to her, propped against the stone wall with tired, fearful eyes.

"What is it?" she barked, haranguing her fear.

"They've... they've completely destroyed the gate mechanism, ma'am... it's... it's ruined..."

The guard gestured to the metal contraption wedged into the stone next to them, and the small gears that were nestled within.

The intruder's dagger had embedded itself between the lever and the main cog almost perfectly – and, as the mechanism had reversed itself to try and close the gate again, the blade had grinded against them and torn the gears to shreds.

Fuck, the sentinel thought, studying the broken hilt of the dagger still wedged against the lever. *That means there's no way of closing the gate without manually resetting the gears.* She released the pressure on the intruder's back and pinched the bridge of her nose, sighing at length until her lungs felt like shrivelled prunes.

Fuck, fuck, fuck—

"Ma'am?"

She turned back to the guard. "What?"

"Why would they want to keep the gate open? Why would they do that?" He asked it so delicately, with his small-boy eyes and his innocent, spot-poked cheeks. He couldn't have been more than sixteen-winter's old, by the look of him.

He's no older than my own son, she realised, unsure of whether to smile or cry.

"I'm not sure why exactly…" she replied, looking from the ruined machinery to the intruder at her feet. She placed a hand on the cowl covering their face and pulled it back slowly. "But I have a feeling it's something to do with what's going on out in the bay…"

The audible gasp from the guard next to her expressed her thoughts better than she could, laying eyes on the intruder's face beneath the black cowl. Their skin was pale and sickly, as if all the life had been drained from it and replaced with a thick black tar. Fang-like incisors dripped blood from their open mouth, and stained the darkness in their eyes with an ugly shade of purple. A black mark like a raven's feather peeled up under one eyelid, flecked with tiny droplets, and across their neck all the way down to their collarbone, the long streaks of ancient knife wounds furrowed the skin there, more than she thought it possible for any one person – or *creature* – to survive.

What the fuck even are you? the sentinel thought with a growing disquiet in her chest. She lifted to her feet with her eyes still fixed on the scars, unable to tear herself away. *Why are you people here?*

"Is... is that a...?"

"A Tarrazi, yes," the sentinel said to the young guard, who had taken on a shade of taupe not too dissimilar to the body at their feet. "You can tell by their earless scalp, and the black etchings under their eyes." She paused. "That, and the fuck-ugly look they all 'ave that can make your stomach roll."

"I...yea..."

Pushing her chest out, she placed her hands against the parapets and looked west towards the bay, where the fortuitous wall of sea mist retained its undaunting form. There were no signs of any ships or jousting masts passing through the grey; the moon could hardly penetrate its mass to discern between land and sea. But, towards the south, the occasional ripple of orange still illuminated behind the veil, as lone cannons continued to fire and the remnants of battle continued to ebb out. The success of those meagre attacks was unknown, she assessed – and the victor, as it was, remained very far from certain.

We can only hope we come out of this with our lives, she thought, watching a droplet of blood drip down her spear and over the chain links of her gloves.

We've already fucked our dignity, after all.

Sighing, she was alerted to the sound of marching boots growing steadily louder on her right: turning to face it, the sentinel watched the two guards re-emerge from the tower with sweat-sheened foreheads, glowing ghostly in the moon's light. Whether by fear or a severe lack of basic fitness, she wasn't initially sure.

"No sign of any more of 'em, ma'am," one of them spluttered, propped up against the stone doorway. They gestured to the body beneath her. "It came on its own... whate'er it is."

"Thank you, officer," the sentinel replied. "I want both of you watchin' the lower entranceway to the tower for the rest of the night from hereon. Keep an eye on the opposin' alleyways for signs of any movement. We don't want any more of these freaks sneakin' up on us. Am I understood?"

They only managed a nod and a sigh in response, turning languidly from the walkway back toward the spiral staircase, near-enough dragging their swords behind them. She turned her nose up at their dissention.

Lazy bastards.

"Do you think there *will* be any more, ma'am?" the young guard asked her tensely, their pale golden hair twitching like dead grass in the wind. "Do you think?"

She looked at him for a long while after he had spoken, mesmerised by his quiet features and his delicate, infantile voice. *You've got my son's hair, too,* she acknowledged with a smile, almost wanting to reach out and touch it, so light and wispy as it was—

She blinked hard once and ground her jaw, digging her nails into her palms almost as punishment. Any sentimentalities she possessed were buried almost as quickly as they had risen.

"I don't expect so, no," she proclaimed. "This one here was most likely a saboteur" – she kicked the body at her feet – "and came here in the event that the Tarrazi actually make it this far and need a way into the main city. But, as they've lost the element of surprise, I have a feeling we won't be seeing any more of 'em for the rest of the night."

The boy took in her words like medicine: sour-tasting and sickly but ultimately helpful. He nodded gently to himself. "I... yea, I hope not, ma'am."

She kept her eyes locked to the horizon, nodding slowly.

For your sake, my dear boy, I hope not too—

"Ma'am!"

A voice, calling out from below: the sentinel frowned and took a step forward, peering down over the walkway's blocky turrets like a vulture.

There, the sentinel caught the eye of a heavily-armoured guards-man stood adjacent to three others, with his helmet in the crook of his arm. His thick head of hair shimmered impressively in the low light, and the steel plates of his suit were so large they could have fashioned their own shields. She had no idea how long they had been stood there, or what their plan was.

"Yes, officer?" the sentinel called in reply, looking between the head guard and the other lackies next to him.

"Ah, ma'am, um... is there a reason why the gate has been opened?" he asked, trying to keep his voice level and unaccusatory. "I mean, we were expecting it to be closed all night, was all... and with whatever's going on in the harbour, well..."

The sentinel clenched a fist, crunching her neck. "The gate should not be open, no. A Tarrazi managed to sneak in through the tower and disable the lever. It's stuck open now I'm afraid."

As soon as the word *'Tarrazi'* left her mouth, the guardsman's eyes seemed to bulge in their sockets, and the other three figures looked up to her with a ghoulish discontent.

"I am begging pardon, ma'am... but did you say, *Tarrazi?*"

"Yes, officer... who the fuck else do you think is currently blowing our ships to smithereens out in the harbour? It's not a training exercise."

He bristled at that, clamping a hand around the pommel of his sword. "Should... should we engage, then, ma'am? If there are Tarrazi troops nearby then—"

"Absolutely fuckin' not," she commanded, letting it be heard by everyone in the vicinity. "Because we need you lot 'ere, defending the gate, in the unlikely-but-let's-not-test-our-fucking-luck chance that the Tarrazi are successful in their little excursion, and manage to get a sizeable force rallied down the street there." She gestured to the wide road leading to the harbourfront ahead. "So no, officer, I do not want you to engage: I want you and your comrades to blockade that gate entrance until reinforcements arrive, and make sure no other bastards find a way through our defences. I'm not taking any chances... am I understood?"

The head guardsman looked up to her blankly, trying to make

sense of the decision she'd made and the implications it had on his next move. Eventually he just nodded his head, frowning dumbly into the open air, before he puffed out his chest and asserted himself once more, every bit the soldier he pretended to be.

"As you wish, ma'am," the guard exclaimed, straightening his back. "We shall remain here and guard the gate until reinforcements arrive, or until the current threat is neutralised and we are safe to proceed."

"Thank you, officer, I'm… most *grateful,*" the sentinel replied, hiding her sigh.

"You have our word that no enemy shall pass this point, and no dangerous entities will enter our great city—"

As his words were cut short, and an arrow impaled him through the eyeball, sending a jet of brain matter spewing from the back of his head.

The sentinel watched him collapse in slow-motion, her skin suddenly crawling with unease.

"*What the fuck…*"

The head guard stared blindly up into the clouds as he fell, clutching towards his face like a cat—

The other soldiers turned to their collapsing leader and gasped, looking to the city beyond the gatehouse with hands reaching for their weapons—

As three more arrows whistled under the city walls, making impact with ferocious speed.

One guard fell with an arrowhead through his throat—

A second lurched backwards, only for the arrow to impale his nostril and pierce his brain like a skewer—

The third dodged the arrow, wheezing and spluttering as they reached for their sword, whimpering at their comrades who now lay dead and stricken over the stone—

Until a figure cloaked in shadow emerged from beneath the gatehouse and ran them through with a jagged blade, digging it deep between their ribs without so much as a whisper.

The sentinel clutched at her spear, bracing against the wall as the scene unravelled beneath her.

She found she couldn't breathe, couldn't think straight.

Her body convulsed—

There are more of them, she gasped, as the dark figure on the ground turned up towards her and flashed a fanged smile.

This was planned all along...

"*Grab your swords!*" she bellowed furiously, knocked from her trance by the hiss of blades being drawn along the walkway beside her. "Make for the street below! Intercept the enemy! *Go!*"

The top of the gatehouse swam with activity suddenly, as the guards streamed around her like enterprising insects. On both sides, her people surged toward the outer towers and disappeared down the spiral stairways, jeering and roaring in a feigned attempt to hide their gnawing fear.

Watching them go, the sentinel looked down on the street again and registered four other figures passing under the gatehouse beneath her, stepping over the arrowed corpses as if they were shit-soaked latrines. They skulked about in a pack, adorned in black robes and black armour, with close-cut crops of hair down the middle of their scalps. The paleness of their skin left no room for interpretation over who they were.

Tarrazi, she spat, her heart in her throat. *The foul fucking bastards...*

"Ma'am," the young guard mumbled fearfully, "are they—"

She pulled the young guard back from the parapets by the shoulders as a number of the Tarrazi looked up towards her, sensing another presence nearby. The flash of their hallowed faces caught in her mind for a moment, stained to the back of her eyelids when she blinked.

Pale faces... pointed fangs...

"There... there are more of them..." the young boy – *man* – whimpered, pushing into her like a frightened fawn. "There are more..."

"Yes, there are, there are," she replied, holding him close.

"But… but you said there wouldn't be—"

"Forget what I said." She gripped his shoulders in both hands and looked him dead in the eyes. "You *must* stay here, you understand? Do not follow me. Do not engage. Do not play a fucking hero. You stay here, and you live, my so—my boy… you got that?"

He nodded at her, muttering and mumbling under his breath. His big, glowing eyes looked almost like a pup's in the moonlight.

"Stay safe," she whispered – pleaded – releasing him and turning towards the tower, counting the prayers in her head that he would live and be alright, and see another day afterwards.

He looks so much like him…

She vaulted through the tower door and down the spiral staircase with a powerful agility, using her spear to spin around corners in a steady quarter-turn. The orange light of the sconces flushed as she went past, carrying a wind at her back like billowing sails. She counted the stairs as she went down, recalling memories of doing so when she had been a child of the army: thinking the steps were massive, and the tower was as big as the mountains in the west. Looking back on it then, everything had seemed impressive to her. She marvelled at just how whimsical life had been as a child, when it hadn't been stacked with personal anxieties and the reality of a soldier's life. As a child, reaching the top of the tower had been the most important thing in her life.

And, as she scrambled down the last flight of stairs to the open door, she wondered if she'd ever get that same bliss again.

Entering out into the cold night air once more, she paced toward the gatehouse and squinted at the moonlight glancing off the stones. A cool wind drifted through the alleyways to her right like a serpent, licking up against her back in agitated waves, and the distinct smell of smoke and ignition powder burned softly in her nostrils.

The guards that had come down before her had formed up in a line next to the tower, which fanned out effortlessly to let her through the middle as she approached. Studying them as she passed, she saw their expressions were ones of dutifulness and unease, stood with swords wavering in front of them and steel caps pulled tight around their ears. A few of them tapped their fingers on hilts and thigh-guards, sweating with anticipation.

And, looking at this lot before us, I can see why they're afraid.

There were seven of them in total, stopped in a semi-circle just past the gatehouse, spread out over the main street in random positions. They lurched about in the dim night like subterranean ghouls, who had risen to the surface to pick away at the scraps and savage any fool who crossed their path. Scratching and clawing; festering in the dark. Representing all things foul and miserable.

Making merry in the blood of the innocents.

Although that wasn't what drew the sentinel's attention in that moment: between them, she spied a strange cloth sack sprawled out across the stone slabs, like a clot of congealed blood swelling in the dark. It held the attention of every Tarrazi present, and appeared to be the reason why they had come to a halt in the first place – but what purpose it served, and what importance it held, the sentinel could only guess.

As she approached, two of the Tarrazi were making difficult work of picking the sack up again, with a third stood facing away from her shouting commands at them in a foreign tongue. It was an individual that she assumed was most-likely their leader, and one who was none-too happy at that.

This can't be all there is, she thought idly, drawing to a stop. *A group of misfit Tarrazi with a bag of loot... and a saboteur who died just to get this gate open for them. How long could've they been in the city before now? And how did they even get in in the first place?* She rolled her tongue over her teeth. *It doesn't make sense... this can't be all there is.*

Unless there is something more serious happenin' further south, and these lot are just opportunists lookin' to make a quick bit of coin from the spoils.

Clasping her spear in both hands, she lifted it over her head like a priest at the altar, and brought the blunt end down against the stones at her feet with an almighty *clang* of metal.

Opposite her, the Tarrazi who had been barking the orders

seemed to sigh with frustration, and turned on her with a simmering rage just behind his eyes.

Suppose we better find out what this really is.

And what you're really doing with that loot…

"By order of the King and the laws of Casantri, I ask that you stand down and dispossess yourselves of your weapons, or face any consequences that may follow," the sentinel proclaimed, levelling her spear. The other guards at her back did likewise, invigorated by her confidence.

The Tarrazi opposite her – a lean figure with a chiselled jaw and a single braid of hair down the middle of their scalp – scratched at their neck and smirked devilishly. Their lips parted to offer an answer.

"No."

The sentinel frowned. "No?"

"No…" they repeated, staring her down. "Do you not understand the common vernacular surrounding refusal to oblige orders, or something?"

The entire line of guards behind the sentinel shuddered at his words; the grip around her spear-pole tightened.

He speaks Provencian…

"Well, luckily for you, I do have a good grasp of such expressions, so allow me to explain it a bit *clearer* for you," the Tarrazi continued, taking a single step forward. "We shall not be dispossessing ourselves of any weapons, nor shall we be handing ourselves over to any authorities – be it you or the city guard – following such dispossess-ions. We have no interest in your orders or dictations, or whatever code it is that you people follow. It doesn't interest us one bit." He paused. "And I believe – and correct me if I'm wrong – that you Provencians have a rather succinct term for the kind of expression I'm offering…"

He gave a callous grin, bearing his fangs.

"…*get fucked.*"

She bared her teeth, repulsed by his serpentine demeanour. "Do not disrespect us… I won't ask again."

"And I won't warrant you another response... when the one I gave was so adequate." He turned from her, back towards the two Tarrazi who had managed to lift the cloth sack in one piece. "Now, if you will kindly excuse us, we shall be taking our cargo and departing your squalid little harbour in good haste... so, my thanks for your introductions, but I would kindly advise you from hereon out to *keep out of our fucking way.*"

The venom dripped off his tongue like a viper, and the sentinel found herself wavering on the spot.

What the hell even is this...

The leader of the Tarrazi gave a whistle, and the black-armoured figures around him all shifted in unison, moving off down the street toward the harbourfront in the distance—

"Stop there, or we open fire!" the sentinel bellowed, surprising herself as much as her guards with the power of her voice.

Opposite her, glazed in moonlight, the Tarrazi leader ground his heels against the stone and hissed, before rounding on her like a storm-cloud. The other Tarrazi around him stopped as well, awaiting their next orders.

"You will lay down your weapons," the sentinel said slowly, "and we shall return your stolen cargo to its various owners in due time. We are a city of law, not a land for the lawless, and this is by decree of the imperial council itself—"

"I *wouldn't* do that if I were you," the Tarrazi growled, pacing like a wolf in the low light. "I *really* wouldn't..."

"You cannot threaten us, *Tarrazi.*"

"I don't need to threaten you, *Zoltha*... I need you to learn your lessons when I *give* them."

"And I need you to lay your weapons *down* and step away from the *cargo.*"

The Tarrazi lifted his hands, grinding his jaw together. Something changed in his aura suddenly: a shift towards accommodation. "Now, I assure you, that won't be necessary. You see, we appear to have an honest misunderstanding—"

A muffled cry broke the night air, stinging her ears.

The sentinel locked eyes with the Tarrazi, whose neck tensed like the trunk of a tree.

What was that...

She looked past him suddenly, out towards the other Tarrazi, and caught sight of the cloth sack as one of the soldiers gave it a vicious kick, ramming their boot deep beneath the fabric—

Where something spluttered and coughed violently, before falling silent once more.

She blinked; she frowned.

The world seemed to freeze before her.

A flash of light crossed the Tarrazi leader's black eyes, studying her intently.

This isn't just... petty thievery, the sentinel realised, far too late.

This is a... kidnapping...

She lifted her spear in her hands, dumbstruck by the revelation, as the other guards looked around at each other wondering what to do.

There was a body in the sack before them. A human life was being stolen away. They had no idea who it was, or where they had come from, or how the enemy had even got their hands on them in the first place. The coldness of reality pressed in on all sides, threatening to overwhelm them where they stood.

The sentinel opened her mouth to form a rallying cry, thinking of her boy and the innocent young man up on the walkway, and her own childhood long ago climbing the tower with big steps—

Missing the shape of the Tarrazi leader as they coiled up like a viper and ran her through with his sword, spearing it up between her armour with a vicious snarl.

"*So much for good graces,*" the Tarrazi growled, leaning in close to her ear. "*We'll have to settle for good riddance instead...*"

She longed to cry – to scream and bellow and wail and sing – but nothing came to her in the end.

A warmth filled her body, crawling over her skin, like the memories of her boy's cherished face and the songs she had sung to him long ago. Happy memories, and full memories. Things she cherished, and had never forgotten.

He had been dead for two years, she knew, taken by a disease with no name in the depths of a perilous winter. It had come and gone without warning; it had left her without any answer. Not a day had passed where she hadn't thought of him, or grieved for him in some way. The boy up on the walkway had been the closest she'd come to seeing him again, but even she knew it wasn't enough.

So, as the light faded from her eyes, staring into the soul-less pits of the Tarrazi before her, all she found the strength to do was smile. Thinking of her boy; thinking of his delicate golden face.

I'll see you soon, my son, she thought.

And then all was dark again.

VIII

The Abductor

These Zoltha sure know how to waste my time, Ë'zo growled, as he pulled the blade from the woman's chest and shoved her over. She slapped down on the stones beneath with a cloudiness in her eyes, gazing up lifelessly at the line of guards who had watched her demise in horror.

Ë'zo scoffed at them and wiped the blood from his blade.

If only they could learn their lessons.

Somewhere behind him, a scream went up, followed by the clatter of marching boots as the *Zoltha* guards descended on the Tarrazi, driven by a lust for revenge and a blind, merciless fury. The Tarrazi responded with equal force as they approached, drawing their blades to form a perimeter around the cloth sack that had been dumped unceremoniously on the floor, hoping to steer the enemy clear and open up a channel for their escape.

This is less than desirable, Ë'zo admitted, turning back to the row of guards stood trembling before him. Ignoring the corpse strewn at his feet, the Tarrazi opened his hands out to get their attention, which only ended up spooking them even more.

He managed a sigh.

How pathetic.

"Now, *Zoltha*... let us be reasonable here," Ë'zo began, rolling a tongue over his pointed teeth. "Please understand what you've been presented with. Your leader is dead... and your friends behind me? They will shortly follow. Neither of them respected my commands;

neither of them backed down when the offer was given. And now, because of that, they will pay the price of it with their blood." He paused, smirking. "So, let us not be hasty with what happens next, and risk succumbing to the same *mistakes*... hm? That would be rather distasteful – wouldn't you agree?"

He looked between each face to gauge their reactions, balancing on the fine line between negotiation and violence. The guards behind him had made their choice between the two outcomes.

Those stood before him, however, were as yet undecided.

"You see, this hold-up you've caused... it's a damning and fruitless waste of my time," Ë'zo continued, as a trickle of blood slipped beneath his glove and slid slowly down his forearm. "I have parameters I need to meet, and a timescale I have to follow. And instances like this" – he gestured behind him, where one of the *Zoltha* guards was cut down the middle and stood gargling their own blood – "do nothing to help that precious timescale, y'see? So, if you people could be oh-so kind and dispatch with any notions of violence you may have, and take on board the advice I gave your leader before her... *less than savoury* demise, then we can find a solution to this that benefits everyone." He paused, nodding his head. "And, as I am feeling rather *benevolent*... I'll even let you keep your lives—"

One of the guards wailed and charged forwards suddenly, catching everyone by surprise, swinging their sword blindly at him—

Ë'zo had enough time for a sigh, before he rammed his fist into the woman's gut and doubled her over, forcing a thin gobbet of spit from her mouth that dangled like a silkworm. A heartbeat later, and he brought his sword pommel down against the back of her head, sending her sprawling onto the stones next to her dead leader without a bead of sweat leaving his body.

Stupid Zoltha.

Taking a moment to compose himself, he turned back to the guards in silence. A strained breath rasped through his lips; a quiet fury leaked through his veins.

"*Now,*" he barked, squaring his jaw, "let us be *fucking reasonable* here—"

The other four guards lifted their spears and swords, flashing their teeth with a dogged determination that made Ë'zo's blood boil. Regardless of his threats, they stood to challenge him, defying him with their very presence. They had watched their leader die, and their comrade fail; they were watching countless other *Zoltha* fall in the blood-soaked streets behind him—

And yet you fight on regardless... you ignorant, fathomless people, Ë'zo spat, looking up to the night sky and the silver round of the moon. Part of him wondered in that moment if the gods were testing him, facing down his mortal enemy in a battle longer than history.

Doing their damnedest, as always, to waste my fucking time—

Two of the guards advanced on him simultaneously, one with a lowered spear and the other with a raised steel blade.

Ë'zo grappled the spear in one hand as it lunged and yanked on it violently, forcing the guard to stumble—

As he swung his blade across to catch the other soldier's sword and slapped it away, turning from the spearman and stepping into the swordman's circle—

Where he snarled and rammed his head forward, breaking the man's fragile nose against his skull to send him spiralling away—

Opening up space to attack the spearman on the other side, who had found their footing and grappled their spear and—

Received an elbow to the cheek for their efforts, twisting away in pain as Ë'zo planted a foot against their arse and kicked them to the floor, dispossessing them of their spear as they fell.

The Tarrazi leader took in a long breath and crunched the bones in his neck.

I tried to warn you people...

Ahead, the other two soldiers advanced, jostling with their blades as the one with the bloodied nose made her recovery, readying a fresh attack—

Ë'zo cut across on one side and then diced through on the other, counterattacking against one of them and carving a nasty trench in their arm—

Before navigating three subsequent strikes, pressing back on his heel to keep steady—

As his sword twisted suddenly, smacking a blade away from his head, forcing the advantage as he stepped in close with his blade menacing and—

Carved across the guard's stomach with a flash of his fangs, as the chainmail scraped open and the guard's face went pale.

Blood spewed down their front like a broken dam, coating their legs in a foul stream of red. Their mouth hung agape, collecting flies and dripping spit as the vital organs that had once occupied their stomach started spilling out of the wound like a skinned snake—

Ë'zo wasted no time – he didn't even waste a breath, in the end. He stepped back effortlessly, curling his nose up, and slung his sword across his body. The dark blade flashed through the air with a sheen of moonlight, and slit the man's throat where he stood, sending him crashing down to the mud where he belonged.

Bloody fucking Zoltha, the Tarrazi growled, looking up with murderous intent.

Bloody fucking feckless Zoltha...

Ahead of him, the other guards he had felled made their slow recovery, suitably humiliated but never lacking conviction. The guard he had kicked to the floor had sidled awkwardly to their feet with their spear in-hand; the man with the broken nose had stemmed the blood flow and snarled toward him again with reddened teeth; the one with the slit in his arm had swapped the blade to the other hand, manipulating it just as strongly despite it being their second choice. Ë'zo found himself smiling.

How about that...

The ambidextrous one stepped forward first, carving across their body in a succession of attacks that Ë'zo knocked aside with some delight, enjoying the first piece of swordsmanship he had seen all night—

A prospect that was immediately ruined by the approach of the spearman, whose initial jab put the Tarrazi off balance and forced him to reconsider his approach—

Before the guard with the broken nose stepped in laboriously and lunged towards his midriff.

Ë'zo snarled in frustration – whispering a hallowed *'fuck this'* under his breath – and, as the sword came towards him, he grabbed it by the thick of its blade, praying his chainmail was strong enough to stop it slicing his fingers apart—

As he clamped his grip and snapped his teeth, tearing the sword from the man's hand to use it as a makeshift bludgeon, swinging it across to catch the ambidextrous man across the face—

Forcing him back—

Forcing a cry between his lips—

Opening up space for Ë'zo to drop the *Zoltha's* blade and step in with his own—

And run the other guard through with his sword, tearing the vertebrae out of their spine.

Ë'zo withdrew his weapon and spat on the corpse as it fell, their mumbling mouth hanging aghast like the caverns of a sea cave. The Tarrazi then turned to the other two guards and snarled in challenge, noting their hesitancy and the tight grip on their steel.

"You look scared, gentlemen!" he bellowed, shifting from a smile to a grimace. The sword felt warm and enticing in his hand.

You should be scared...

The sounds of suffering echoed out from the street behind him; the sea wind rasped through the alleyways and whispered all around.

Whether by judgement, or the drive of blind fear, the two guards advanced on Ë'zo at the same time, bellowing and swearing with their steel glinting against the moon.

Their boots clattered against the stone slabs. The jangle of chain-mail knocked in their ears.

The Tarrazi breathed deeply and lowered into a stoop, balancing the blade against his shoulder.

A heartbeat passed—

The spearman lunged—

The other guard swiped up—

Ë'zo allowed himself a smile—

As his blade slid across his left, twisting into a lunge to his right, and a silence followed that even the gods shivered at, in their vast gilded caves high above.

Ahead of him, the guard with the sword fell to their knees, slumped with their head resting on their collar to hide the massive gouge that now constituted their windpipe.

To his right, the spearman relinquished their weapon, letting it clatter to the floor as they reached up to their throat and grabbed at the blade embedded there, spewing blood like a delta over their armour and down into the rivets of their chest.

And behind him, a dead silence echoed out, as the surviving Tarrazi in front of the gatehouse turned to their leader and regarded his work, which now littered the floor at his feet in ugly, contorted piles. It was the masterpiece of a killer. The ruin of man.

Death will always follow.

Ë'zo flicked his sword from the spearman's neck and rose to a stand, letting the body topple forwards in a splash of putrid blood. Taking a breath, he turned and cleaned his blade off, approaching his kin who stood amongst their own perilous slaughter, regarding him quietly in the gloom.

Well... now that this mess is over, maybe we can finally get back to the task at hand, the Tarrazi leader thought with some chagrin. *We have wasted far too much time as it is, after all.*

And I shall not be the one to keep her Highness waiting.

Ë'zo approached the survivors and slid his sword back into its sheath, his gaze passing from corpse to corpse littering the floor beneath them.

"How many dead?" he asked plainly, looking to the first Tarrazi he could find.

"Seven of enemy... two of kin," they replied, lowering their gaze. There was a deep slice from the edge of their eye down to their jaw, which had a dry stream of blood snaking down to their shoulder. "Their fates were noble of *feduzak*... the gods take them gladly in Their arms."

"Then may we bless their passage into the next life, and hope *Kand'u* is merciful to them when they arrive in His arms."

In unison, the Tarrazi bowed their heads and slapped their forearms three times over, invoking the gods and exulting their kin in their passage to the heavenly realms. A dark cloud passed across the moon as they prayed, mirroring the sombreness below.

"However, this is no time for grief... let us not linger where the dead make rest," Ë'zo declared, gesturing toward the cloth sack sprawled out on the stone to his right. "We still have a duty to our Queen... and time is running out to fulfil her aims. We must deliver on what we have promised..."

And pray for her mercy when we arrive.

With an eerie whistle from their leader, the Tarrazi formed up around the cloth sack in a neat arrowhead, with two soldiers hefting the stolen cargo and making off down the thoroughfare toward the sea. Ë'zo positioned himself to one side of them, flanking the merchant houses on the right where the *Zoltha* were most likely to emerge, keeping a hand locked to the pommel of his sword at all times. They had been caught out by the enemy once thus-far.

He made no intention of allowing that again.

Overhead, the sky swirled and vibrated, dashed with the dull purple hues of a fast-approaching dawn and the grey streaks of smoke from distant, blooming fires. Clouds coiled about each other like writhing snakes, consuming the moon for long stretches and casting the world beneath in shadow. It was ominous, almost, as the Tarrazi shifted in a pack down the long street, facing down the threat of a storm with only their mettle to keep them safe. The sky looked embittered, and enraged; their composure held nonetheless.

But once the first spots of rain began falling, dashed with the distant rattle of thunder, even that fortuitous composure began to wash away.

"A storm... rising," one of the Tarrazi muttered under their breath, pulling their cowl further over their brow.

Ë'zo smirked, lifting his face to the open skies and letting the rain wash over it. "This is no storm, *feduzak*... this is a test," he said almost as a whisper, the sky above like churning waves. "We have angered their Mother, and forsaken Her ways... and what swirls above us now, threatening to wash us away, is an example of the power She holds. This is not our land, after all, and what we have taken was never ours to have."

Out of the corner of his eye, he saw the Tarrazi frown. "What mean... what is mother?"

The question came with such innocence, entirely unknowing. A question from a Tarrazi soldier who lived to serve and do as they were told; a soldier who saw the black and the white, without any estimation of the grey between. The nuances of the wider world, and the history that had shaped it, were beyond the realms of what they considered important in their mortal life.

And perhaps you would be right, Ë'zo thought with a sigh.

Were this world simple and mortal in the first place.

"The Mother of Provenci, *feduzak*... the assistant to the All-Mother, the Great Being of this land, may She bless us," he explained. "One of four original Mothers, scattered across the Ice-breaker Sea..."

"Mothers... like ones from stories... *skal* stories."

"Yes, exactly. From the stories, yes: *'through their voice, the All-Mother speaks; by their hand, the All-Mother guides'*... and so on and so on, yes."

"Stories... are real?" the Tarrazi asked.

"Well, in a sense, yes: the Mothers are real, and they are here among us, dictating the whim of the All-Mother to those of us worthy enough to hear it." He scoffed, shaking his head. "I mean, most of the time that means they don't give a shit about us, and mutter in the ears of our rulers without restraint... but *sometimes*, when the darkness rears its brutish head and threatens to consume all things, they have the guts *at last* to finally act…"

He looked to the sky, snorting without fear.

"… even if that means just a little rain…"

Enticingly, Ë'zo opened his mouth and slid his tongue over his fanged teeth, letting the droplets of rain splash against it and slide down into his throat. It was cool and refreshing, stinging his neck like needles.

"Should we… we fear?" the soldier inquired, studying him.

"No, no… there's nothing to fear in all this. Their Mother can't hurt us, really."

"But how… how you know?"

Ë'zo stepped over to the Tarrazi and placed a hand on their shoulder, smiling putridly. "Because we had our own Mother once, long ago… and in our dying breaths as a people fifty years ago, She was taken from us, never to return. We lost Her, and we lost ourselves too, as the *Zoltha* came up from the south and colonised our homes, crushing us under their boot with their callous, despotic ways." He spat the word of the enemy, evicting the sourness it left on his tongue. "But, in time, the world rebalances, and the wheels of time do turn. Power stirs… and rewrites our history." He lifted his hand, pointing to the sky above. "These clouds, and this storm, and the Mother's *rage* it embodies… none of this is done to challenge us, you see. It is not done to hurt us, or break us down. No… it is done instead, out of *fear*. It is done, because the very balance of this world, and the lives of those people we bathe in the blood of… are under threat. Because they are all *afraid* of who we are, and what we have become. They fear us… as we once feared them." He smiled. "Because although we have no Mother anymore, and we have fallen from our true path… it is another who now guides us, and shall lead us to triumph as we tear this nation up from its roots, and bleed it over our soil. Another soul; another power. She is Grief, and she is Wrath; she is Sorrow and Sin, and Ruin. All shall cower before her in the end…"

He looked up to the skies, with light in his eyes.

All shall hail her Majesty, the Iron Queen…

Above them, the moon broke through the clouds for a moment, lustrous and radiant, spilling out through the mist and smoke clogging the horizon by the sea. It seemed to intertwine with the darkness there, forming knots like woven thread, and for a brief heartbeat a woman's face appeared through the clouds, surveying the world below.

It was an apparition, with a scarred skull and haunting pale eyes, looking down on the Tarrazi in the street. She flashed her teeth, running a serpentine tongue over them, savouring the taste of powder smoke on her lips. Her gaze shifted, unblinking, across the bay and the waters of the harbourside wall: serpents crawled up her neck, hissing and spitting, as dragon fire billowed within the darkness behind, illuminating her visage torturously.

The other Tarrazi on the street alongside them – with their heads held low, sheltering against the rain – didn't see the mirage that crept through the clouds in that moment, expanding across the sky overhead. They didn't even realise it was there at all, such was their determination to get out of the harbour in one piece.

But for Ë'zo, and the lone Tarrazi soldier stood alongside him, the sight they witnessed above them drew fear and awe from their hearts, kindling a ferocious purpose in their souls that not even the rain could wash away.

"She is everywhere, *feduzak,*" Ë'zo said in wonder. "Everywhere, always, with us…"

They gazed up and looked on, entirely lost in the glinting eyes and terrifying power of the figment above – until a *boom* of thunder crackled over the sea, forcing the moon back into the shadows, and the apparition of their Queen fell away like dust, stained onto their minds forevermore.

Ë'zo blinked once, and turned his focus back to the wide street ahead, with the faint impression of the woman in the clouds forming behind his eyelids. *She makes herself known to us, and reminds us how close she is to us. At our backs and behind our eyes.*

hundreds of miles away in reality.

Ahead of the Tarrazi soldiers, a few old outbuildings marked the end of the street, stood aloft like strange statues in the broken light. Ë'zo saw there an old fishing hut and the wide wooden doors of a boathouse, alongside the spindly struts of a loading crane just to one side. They marked the very edge of the harbour wall, beyond which stood nothing but the swollen sea and the long wooden pontoons jutting out into the bay like fingers. To the south of that lay a mass of broken ship hulls and the bodies of dozens of soldiers; to the north, an unrepentant sea mist marked the horizon as far as one could see.

And somewhere in between it all, on an unassuming pontoon by the harbour wall, a longboat lay moored inconspicuously in the dark, offering the Tarrazi a one-way passage up the coast, back to the sprawling wastes they called home.

"We're getting close, *feduzak*!" Ë'zo called out, as a number of the Tarrazi soldiers knocked their hands against their chests. "I can smell our homeland already!"

A few cheers went up amongst them, addled with exhaustion and the sheer desire to get home in one piece. They swayed as they walked, approaching the end of the long street at last, their legs bowed and stumbling like newly birthed fawns. Ë'zo looked out over them with a burgeoning pride in his chest, commending his people for their perseverance, satisfied in the knowledge that they would be handsomely rewarded with goods and graces for their tribe. They deserved as much, after sneaking into the city the previous day and assailing the palace keep that night. Their work had been rife with dangers, and death was always knocking, but in the end they had come out of the fire alive, ready for the long passage home.

The Tarrazi leader took a deep breath, and found himself wanting to go over to each one of them and give his thanks, showing his appreciation for their stoic efforts—

When shouts echoed out from the alleyways on both sides, and streams of *Zoltha* soldiers charged between the houses towards them.

Ë'zo tensed up and went for his blade.

A shudder went through his kin.

We weren't expecting company.

"*Zoltha,* both sides!" one of the Tarrazi bellowed, whipping his blade from its sheath. "We… we must—"

"Everyone *keep moving!*" Ë'zo bellowed into the cold air, straining the muscles in his neck. "Pick up the pace, you *bastards!* Get to the longboat before they intercept us!"

He reached out and shoved the nearest Tarrazi to make his point, pressing them on towards the rickety boathouse ahead. He shouted and he hollered, spitting fire into the wind. Metallic clatters and Provencian cries scattered through the air around him. Their escape plan relied on his momentum, and the tenacity of the Tarrazi people. They had only just recovered from one near-fatal incident by the gatehouse.

And I'm not about to stumble headlong into another one.

Ë'zo turned on his heel, pushing the last of the Tarrazi forward as the first *Zoltha* soldiers spilled from the alleyway at their back, streaming out like a flood of rats escaping a putrid sewer. There were dozens of them, charging in from both sides, with enough steel to stock an armoury for months. All gnashing teeth and bellowed commands, more than the surviving Tarrazi could ever hope of fending off—

Ë'zo turned, his stomach a fierce knot of anguish, and started running.

The others did likewise around him, picking up the pace in unison – even those poor souls who bore the weight of their cargo, as it swung haphazardly between them like a jump-rope.

The old boathouse rose up alongside them, with busted windows on the upper floor and a number of fishnets draped across the angular walls. The sea breeze swept up across the bay against the building's east side, buffeting the Tarrazi as they skirted along its edge and passed it by without a thought, slipping under its alcoves with the frantic scurrying of mice. The entire building seemed to leer towards them as they passed, intrigued by the happenings of the harbour that night, as the cannon-fire in the wider bay drew still and the sound of marching steel boots shook its very foundations—

"*Move!* Keep moving!" Ë'zo wailed, sensing the prickles of sweat down his spine as the enemy closed in on them. There were so many of them; the Tarrazi were so few. "Down the stairway, get on the pontoon *now!*"

The harbourside spread out before them suddenly as they passed the last line of houses, stretching impossibly wide to either side as far as their black eyes could see. There were lapping waves and screeching crows and the groaning creaks of wooden struts. A wall of mist hung around the headlands to the north; and to the south, a dour, smoky greyness ate at every inch of the world. There were no signs of any Tarrazi ships, and there was no cannon-fire ringing out across the bay. All that remained was an eerie stillness, coated in streaks of moonlight.

A stillness that was about to be upended by bloodshed, and the deadly clatter of steel blades.

The Tarrazi soldiers piled down the wooden steps of the nearest pontoon, stretching out from the harbour wall just passed the old boathouse. It groaned under their weight, the supporting pillars below straining to hold them aloft. The churning waters were already alive with the bodies of carnivorous fish, and the terrifying toothy mouths of huge lampreys. They jostled amongst each other and slapped against the pillars wildly, insatiable and monstrous, demanding their toll in blood from the stumbling Tarrazi above. Ë'zo only allowed himself a glance down over the edge – spying the silver, slithering shapes there – before his sense and his stomach got the better of him and he returned quickly to the task at hand.

We aren't going to survive this, came his first thought: the first real, tangible thing he had comprehended since the *Zoltha* had appeared. *We can't survive this. Even if we get the cargo into the boat... and ready the oars in time... we'll all be dead by the time we set off. They'll reach us and overwhelm us, and then we're all fuckin' dead and this was all a massive waste.*

The gut-wrenching finale of our beautiful master plan… upended because we couldn't load a fucking boat in time.

He hissed and spat; he bellowed at his people to keep moving, to survive just a little while longer. He clawed for answers and escape routes that weren't there and couldn't be there. Praying to whichever god was listening for their salvation. Knowing the futility of it – the blindness of it – waiting for a miracle as everything came crashing down—

Wait.

Ë'zo ground to a halt, his eyes like wandering fires, and turned to face the enemy advancing towards them.

Alongside him, another brutish Tarrazi did likewise, looking between him and the *Zoltha* soldiers with an expression of unhinged panic.

"What… what is it? What's…"

Ë'zo ignored him: with a quick glance – and a moment's reprieve – he peered over the edge of the pontoon to the thrashing waves below—

And a smile coiled over his face, wicked and most foul.

"Your axe, *feduzak*," he boomed, extending his arm out.

The Tarrazi looked baffled. "Wha—"

"Give me your *fucking weapon!*"

Ë'zo snatched it from the soldier's hand and hefted it in his arms: a beautiful steel pole-axe with a mean curved blade at one end, glinting splendidly against the moon. In the low light, he appeared almost like an executioner.

"Go with the others – get the cargo loaded into the longboat. *Now!*"

No further orders were required to that effect: the soldier turned from Ë'zo and launched down the pontoon towards his comrades, leaving the Tarrazi leader out on his own against the encroaching *Zoltha* and their blades.

But, as he stood before them on the pontoon, defiant and proud, Ë'zo offered only a coy grin to their looks of hate and vengeance. He smelt the air and sensed their anger, and a warmth swelled in his chest. He revelled in it, extending the moment as long as he could, staring down his ancient enemy with a furore that had crossed the millennia. It was a destiny that flowed with his blood; it was fused to his very bones. An ancient pact of blood and steel that could not be undone.

The enemy; his enemy.

The enemy of all enemies.

With a single breath, Ë'zo hefted the pole-axe and swung it down beneath the panels at his feet—

Where a powerful *crack* of wood snapped in his ears, as the axe-blade broke the supporting pillar holding the entire structure aloft.

Ë'zo threw the pole-axe down and launched away from the enemy, nearly falling on his face as the entire pontoon lurched and he struggled to keep his footing.

The *Zoltha* at his back continued their charge, entirely ignorant to the broken pillar and the perilous bend in the wood at their feet—

Screeching, suddenly, as the panels shattered beneath them, wrenching the pontoon to one side and tearing a massive hole down its middle—

As the *Zoltha* fell, piling on top of each other, collapsing into the murky depths that were alive with flesh-eating horrors—

With those behind grinding their heels against the panels, grabbing desperately for solid ground, for anything that might hold them aloft and let them survive a while longer—

But it was too late for any of them, in the end.

Far, far too late.

Stepping onto the next section of wood panels – supported by two huge pillars that showed no sign of collapse – Ë'zo let go of a long breath and tried to steady his heart, the heat of the adrenaline still pulling up his spine. He whispered a prayer under his breath – something about mercy and fate – before turning slowly back towards the pontoon behind.

Or what was left of it, that was, after his plan had exacted its toll.

From the harbour wall to the damaged panels a few feet before him, the entire pontoon had toppled over like the folds of a sea anemone, caving in on one side to bring the whole structure down behind it. The waters below furrowed and bubbled with activity, disturbing the steady flow of waves that lapped up against the walls just beyond. There was no sign of any bodies, or even the remains of them; even the silver shapes of the lampreys and fish had disappeared from the surface altogether. There were only the shards of wood panels, and the snapped remains of the pillars.

And the oily slick of human blood, bubbling up from the depths like geysers.

Opposite him, stood along the stone stairway protruding from the harbour wall, the surviving soldiers looked down on the ruin beneath with a look of abject shock. Some of them had survived the carnage, and scrabbled to safety just in time; some of them had stopped at the harbourside in the shadow of the old boathouse, and witnessed the destruction from afar. All had been witnesses, and watched their comrades die.

None who remained could fathom what to do next, as blood welled to the surface below.

Death is death... and now you see it, Ë'zo sneered, as perilous rain fell from the sky and trickled over his scalp. A few of the soldiers opposite glanced up to him, gazing out past the moon at his shadow, but their expressions were no longer those of hate and vengeance: in their place were looks of tiredness and grief, no longer interested in violence or blood.

They've seen enough blood this day to last them a lifetime, he mused, closing his eyes.

Let's hope they take this as their due warning, and don't make the same mistakes again.

Ë'zo turned away from them – leaving the *Zoltha* to their pitiful mourning – to look out on the pontoon beyond, where he hoped his people would be loaded into the longboat and ready to set sail with the cargo stowed away—

Only to find a scene of horror in its place: one that tore the breath from his lungs and stuttered the rhythms of his heart.

What the fuck…

His people – his kin, who had travelled halfway across the world with him – lay dead across the pontoon in shadowy piles, many of them with their hands still grappling their swords. The cloth sack – the whole reason they had endeavoured on the mission in the first place, and sacrificed so many lives against the *Zoltha* – lay hanging from the panels to his right, where the longboat rose and fell slowly on the waves, as if resting on the chest of a giant. The sea mist had closed in across the bay, burying the end of the pontoon in a grey murk that remained completely impenetrable to the eye—

Until a massive figure in a black robe stepped out from the wall of shadow, a twisting black sabre hanging loosely in one hand.

Ë'zo – barely conjuring enough strength to breathe – whipped his sword from its sheath and stooped into a fighter's stance, taking a few steps forward into the outskirts of the mist. His skin was alive, as if tormented by flame, cavorting across his whole body until he felt like exploding. His people were dead; they were all dead. They had died at the hands of a shadow.

A shadow that now stood before him.

"*Who the fuck are you*!" Ë'zo yelled, his anger and terror mixing on his tongue. "Do you have any *idea* what you've just done!"

The shadow loomed before him, stood amongst the corpses of his kin, and said nothing in reply.

"You've ruined *everything*! All our work has been for *nothing*!"

The shadow opposite gave no response: it gave no recognition that Ë'zo had even spoken.

"What the fuck *are you*!"

Still nothing escaped the shadow's lip—

"*I am a redeemer,*" it boomed, both as a whisper and a cannon-blast, knotting tendrils about his heart.

The Tarrazi leader shuddered, feeling the panels rock beneath him. "A… *redeemer*? A redeemer of what?"

"*The time has come. She... has decided. Balance must be restored.*"

"Who has decided? What does that mean——"

"*He must die.*"

The words were like a knife-blade buried deep in his chest, leeching the blood from his body like surgery. Ë'zo looked down at the cloth sack sprawled between them, and felt the grip tighten on his sword.

"No," the Tarrazi blurted. "No, no he cannot... he can't die..."

"*Balance must be restored.*"

"My Queen has demanded him! He must be kept alive... used, for leverage——"

"*The usurper cannot prevail. It is the only way.*"

Ë'zo gripped his sword in two hands, snarling with spittle over his lips, the image of the woman in the clouds burning behind his eyes. "I cannot let you do that. It cannot happen. He must live... I won't let you *kill him!*"

A ripple went through the Tarrazi suddenly, shuddering along the pontoon beneath his feet.

Opposite, the shadow drew the sword across their chest, impossibly dark against the moon, and growled.

"*He must die...*" the figure repeated, flashing their blade.

"*...and you... shall die with him.*"

In a flash of burning light, the figure crossed the distance between them with impossible speed, raising their blade to strike down at Ë'zo before he had even had a chance to assess.

The Tarrazi whipped his sword up, forcing a deflection: the blades chimed together imperiously before slinging apart again.

Another strike came in from the left; Ë'zo brought his sword across to meet it, nearly snapping his wrist with the force of it.

A third attack whipped in on the right, incomprehensibly fast; the Tarrazi could do nothing but lift his arm-guard up in a feigned attempt at a block——

As the huge sabre smacked against Ë'zo's greave, numbing his fingers and rocketing blood up into his shoulder.

A scream escaped his lips.

Bruising swelled over his skin.

His body reeled and his anger rose—

The whole dance began again.

No thought crossed his mind in the subsequent moments. No weakness nor hesitation passed through his brain. The attacks that came were fuelled purely by instinct, and the venomous desire to see the figure before him cut down for what they had done.

Ë'zo struck out, with a devastation that would have dispatched any normal fighter, gritting his teeth and snarling with rage as his sword cut through the mist. Every swing was lethal; every strike was malice. He took steps forward: dangerous steps, advancing into the shadow's circle, forcing them onto the defensive as they rocked back on their heels. Carving down and cutting through, navigating a number of training techniques with each strike, blended with the free-form of wanting a bastard dead as he pivoted and parried and roared.

The figure before him was a mass of black and grey, impossible to decipher. All motion and shadow and darkness. Black robes and a black cowl distorted the image of a face just beyond. Silver glinted as the sabre struck, inviting the attacks with a perilous ease, matching Ë'zo's form – his strength and his agility – almost perfectly.

No fighter of the Known World has the sword-skill to match this, the Tarrazi thought with a ripple of terror. *My people are masters of the blade... it is in our blood; in our very nature. There are no other souls in this present age with a martial skill to match us.*

This... can't be possible.

Pacing down the pontoon amongst the bodies of his kin, Ë'zo continued his stream of attacks without fault, carving down with a ferocity that showed why he had been chosen for the mission in the first place.

But even then, in the hallowed veil of the sea mist, he noticed something in the figure's form that set his heart knocking: every strike he made against his enemy was met with equal force; every step forward into their circle was adjusted for almost immediately; every parry and feint and counter-shift and lunge did nothing to sway the figure's resolve, or open up any space to land a meaningful hit. Instead, they copied his movements and pre-empted his attacks before he had even considered making them. They saw through him, and beyond him, so that they never strayed too close to the edge or lost their footing on the panels. Dancing with him, almost; revelling in the violence and the mastery of the blade. It should have been impossible. All of it should have been impossible.

And yet it isn't.

He swung his sword down, missing their sabre entirely – stepping back as the figure lunged forward, almost impaling his stomach.

I've just run out of luck this time.

Ë'zo lifted his blade over his head, jarring his shoulders against an overhead strike destined to cleave his skull in two.

He lowered his weapon just as fast, catching two levelled swings aiming for his midriff, smacking them both away with a chime of steel, forcing him to backstep once again—

As the figure changed direction and stepped across to the pontoon's edge, catching him off-guard with an unusual lunging blow at the same time—

The Tarrazi leader snapped it against his sword and pressed down against their sabre, staring deep into the darkness beneath the figure's cowl—

"What are *you*!" Ë'zo howled, as rain splattered over his face and fizzed through the mist above his head.

"*I am a redeemer,*" the figure boomed, thunderous and mighty, their voice rattling through his eardrums. "*I am a champion of a lost time, returned to do Their bidding. This is the only way...*"

The figure shoved his sword away and stood opposite him, a few fragile inches from the pontoon's slippery edge.

The ground shuddered at their feet; Ë'zo snarled.

"*...and death... is your only consequence.*"

The shadow stepped forward, entering into Ë'zo's circle as the

Tarrazi leader sliced down, closing his eyes with a bellow—

To open them again moments later, and find nothing there: no sign of the figure or their sabre, or the remnants of their soul—

As a blade carved down the length of his back, tearing through metal and flesh like it was nothing.

Ë'zo gasped, shivering in the mist.

He opened his mouth to speak.

No words followed.

It... it's... impossible...

His legs faltered, buckling at the knees. He stared off blankly into the mist, penetrated by thin reams of moonlight.

It can't be...

He swallowed once, and once only, tasting blood on his tongue.

His final thought being one of disbelief, as he toppled into the waters down below.

IX

The Forgotten

N o bubbles rose, when the water finally lay still. The waves lapped against the pillars without interruption. The moonlight danced across the surface, shimmering like a great sheet of ice.

And the Tarrazi leader, was no more.

Gazing down from the pontoon, the figure regarded the waters below. Acknowledging their stillness. Assessing.

Prevailing—

They stepped away from the edge: from the perilous waters and the silver fish, and the death it carried like a stench. They stepped away from the waters, to regard the other bodies sprawled around them. The bodies and their faces, lying across the panels. The bodies the figure had put there: sent to the mud without a chance to breathe. To even think. Bleeding now, through the panels into the sea. Into the perilous waters amongst the silver fish, the death stench on their bodies.

The figure stepped over them, past them, with hardly a whisper of remorse. Gliding like a wraith, moving between the bodies. The sea mist coiled around them, investigating like the polyps of a curious invertebrate. Pulling around the figure's robes; up under their cowl, hoping to see within—

The figure stopped, gazing down at their feet.

A cloth sack lay there, discarded. It was stained through with seawater, and a few flecks of blood. Straddled between the pontoon and the longboat, jostling with the waves, amongst the dead litter of its captors. All dead and done and forgotten now.

Only the sack remained—

With a single nudge of their boot, the figure rolled the body off the edge of the pontoon and into the longboat. It contorted strangely as it fell, bending in multiple places, depressing the boat against the waves until its upper lip nearly tipped below. The *thud* the sack produced when it landed was odd and unruly.

The groan of pain it produced moments later, was even more so.

The figure lowered their head toward the boat rocking beneath them, acknowledging the noise. The sheer reality of it. Here was a destiny forged by gods.

Bundled in a sack, ready to die.

They stepped from the pontoon's edge, landing in the longboat with a heavy *thud* of boots. It rocked from side to side for a number of moments; the figure stood firmly and settled the vessel beneath their feet. Its agitation on the waters ceased. The waves continued to lap delicately against its small hull. The mist twisted around its prow like an eidolon—

Reaching out with a gloved hand, the figure untrussed the longboat from its moorings and cast them aside.

The vessel immediately caught the waves, rocking away from the pontoon slowly on a series of small, circulating eddies—

The figure stooped low, gnarled and crow-like, withdrawing an oar from within the boat's shadowed interior—

Regarding the arrows that lanced the vessel's hull, puckering it like hairs, as they dipped the paddle into the churning sea waters and pulled back—

To free the longboat from the harbour surf, gliding gently north out of the bay.

Casting the oar into the waters – discarding it, as so many other things had been discarded that night – the figure looked out on the harbourside from the stern of the tiny longboat, and witnessed there a ruin of catastrophic proportions, inflicted by the maker's own fallacy.

The night was falling away, bleeding away to a sullen grey the same colour as slate, interspersed with iron clouds and the ugly, sluggish dregs of smoke pulling off the storehouses in the south. The waters were a deep, blemished blue, like burst veins under the skin, broken occasionally by the white rise of waves and the meandering trails of sea-serpents. The walls were liquid to the eye, glinting with light and seawater, shimmering like scales across the bay as far as the eye could see. They remained the only untainted part of the harbourside that night, devoid of any mark or wound from the indignant barrages of the Tarrazi. Stood resolute and proud, crusted by molluscs and doused by oily blood, they were the survivors of the ordeal that had upturned the world that night. They were the last thing standing, in many ways.

And they would be the first to witness what came next, when the sun rose that fateful day. The first to witness the new beginning, and the end that would surely follow. The sun would emerge like fire and gold on the horizon.

And a cruel reality would dawn with it.

The figure aboard the longboat lowered their head in concession, as the waves churned and the sky rippled and the boat sliced through the waters of the sea. In the deep south beyond, a reddish aura congealed against the distant horizon, where the smouldering fires of buildings and livelihoods continued to burn. Its smoke carried off over the waves, merging with the shroud of heavy sea mist, where the massive, terrifying shapes of Provenci galleons circled in the dark like dogs, brought low with their tails between their legs despite their evident success.

"*No winners,*" the figure boomed, looking from the masts of the huge ships in the distance down to the sack at their feet. They regarded it plainly for a moment, lifeless and uncaring, as if it were nothing more than a bundle of looted goods, unphased by the sheer gravity of what it really was.

"*No winners,*" they repeated, stooping low to look upon it closely.

"*Only war in the end…*"

Delicately, tentatively, like a mother brushing the embryonic fluid from a new-born's eyes, the figure placed a gloved hand on the drawstring of the cloth sack, wrapping it around their fingers.

With the other hand, they pried the small hole apart, loosening the drawstring in tiny increments, revealing the silver rounds of cups and the studded jewels of necklaces to the open sea air, peeling back layer after layer of shadow and gloom—

Until a groan and a whisper escaped the bag.

And eyes that had been blinded, saw once again.

X

The Crown of Omens

From darkness, came light.

The world reborn again.

He awoke from a stupor, both fleeting and centuries-old, his crusted eyes peeling open to look out on the world once more. His skin flushed with sweat and warmth. Rigid objects pressed against his stomach, digging painfully into his back. Something constricted about his neck, bound tightly like a noose.

He looked out through a lens of shadow, closing around his vision like the opening of a porthole. Furrowed at the edges and rough to the touch, it peeled slowly open, revealing the moon of his face to the moon of the sky high above, waning now as it was, streaked in darkness—

With a dark shape slipping away on one side, and an even greater darkness disappeared behind it, hiding away somewhere in the beyond where things were true and clear and real. Had his heart still been connected to his mind, perhaps he would have jumped at the presence somewhere above him. Perhaps his pulse would have raced, or his breath would have caught in his throat. But instead, all that prevailed was an agitated numbness, rising in fits and starts, cloaking his body as if trapped underwater.

He tried to fight against it – to swim against the current – but where his thoughts may have formed, the strength in his limbs did not. He was a statue, it seemed, breathing in husky rasps with a mock-sentience as his body slowly failed him all over again. Caught in a net with no hope of escape.

Somewhere, someone laughed.

He peered out into the beyond, with the sky bleeding black, blue and grey as a precipitous dawn approached. The entrails of clouds lined the air above them, hiding the passage of night and day behind a glossy sheen. It was strange and mesmerising to his old, owl-like eyes, gazing up into the space high above.

And, if he looked close enough, those same clouds could have even been mistaken for smoke—

A weight pressed against the base of his skull, rolling him gently forwards. Some numb, curdling sensation pulled at his chest. His eyes seemed to move with a different momentum to his skull, pushing them back into his sockets, suspending his consciousness as the void rose to meet him again—

And was swept away like a gust of wind just as fast, as his gaze cast across the waters of the beyond, and met the horrors awaiting him there.

A ruin, and a darkness.

Silence.

The echoes of screams.

Broken hulls and broken masts and burning bloated bodies—

Toppled buildings; toppled towers.

Flayed skin.

Fire and smoulder.

Ash.

Death.

It was impossible. It was impossible. It had to be impossible—

And yet it was there, before him, staring at him. Staring through him. Laughing at him.

Someone was laughing. Something, somewhere. Laughter.

Pain. So much pain.

The echoes of violence; the remnants of battle. The harbourside stained with it, weeping from it. Grief-ridden and sorrowful, all bitterness and sin. It should have been impossible.

And yet it had gone so wrong.

He had been there. He had been there, in the city, and then the enemy had come. They had come in the dark, gaiters over their faces, knives in their hands. They had come for him, hunting him like dogs, like wolves even. They had come without a whisper, nor a word.

The cannons had blasted, and they had taken him.

He remembered coldness, and swaying, and sickness. A noxious vapour in his noise, pulling bile across his tongue. It had all come in waves, slipping into and out of a void without any clear reason why. Surrounded by voices and names, and the occasional whip of a steel blade. Violence percolating, exacting all around. All-consuming. Endless.

Evermore.

And the violence had become real to him, at last, staring out across the bay towards the city he called home. The greatest imperial capital of the Known World, brought to its knees in flame. Assailed in the night, by an enemy once-forgotten. Making off with a singular prize.

Gone without a whisper.

He looked towards Casantri, and the smouldering redness on the horizon, and a single tear traced down his cheek. Rolling over the wrinkles of his face, it nestled in the wiry strands of his beard, absorbing back into his skin as if it'd never been born. It was a reminder of a hope, and a world that was now lost. Swept up in the heat of battle.

And run out by the advent of war.

He blinked once, consigning the image to memory, as a great storm clouded his mind. A heartbeat passed, long and trembling—

As the pressure on the back of his head suddenly released.

Laughter chimed in his ears as his head fell, and he couldn't conjure the strength to stop it from falling. It was inevitable, in the end, as a great number of things had sadly become.

He let his eyes roll back in his head as his head fell weightlessly down. He let his gaze pass from the city walls to the sea to the bruise-coloured sky. Numbness swamped his body, coiling up his neck like vines.

The void rose to meet him, softly and soundly, preparing his body for the journey ahead.

The city in the distance – the city he called home – fell away from the world as he did.

In the end there was nothing but shadows. Nothing but darkness, and fire. For the end of the world had come at last.

And from dark ends, come darker beginnings.

ACKNOWLEDGEMENTS

This book is dedicated to my illustrator, Diego Spezzoni.
I met Diego online, while scrolling through hashtags in the hopes of finding a cover artist on social media. At the time, my experience in seeking out creatives online was amateur to the point of being ridiculous – I admit I was only 19, but I had also just written a 550 page dark fantasy, so the point was kind of moot to begin with.
I stumbled upon Diego's dark, gothic artwork – of sacrificial pagans and bull-demons, to name a couple of subjects – almost by accident in the end, and something about it seemed to perfectly align with the equally-dark and arguably-gothic themes that ran through the veins of *The Fangs of War*. I had no idea what I was doing at the time, and if my plan was destined for failure to begin with – so, with my fingers crossed, I contacted Diego in October 2021 asking for him to do a cover design for me.

And the rest, I believe, is history.

Now, writing this nearly two years later, Diego is not only my wonderful illustrator and cover designer: he's also a good friend. He is always up for another project whenever I throw one his way, and produces covers of such jaw-dropping immensity that I can hardly contain my excitement at seeing them.

Despite the motifs of my novels, I am not typically one for believing in fate, but the luck I had in finding such an excellent illustrator for my debut series is something I will forever be astounded by, and of course grateful for.

So, Diego, if you do read this, thank you for everything my friend. You are an incredible artist, and a true gentleman. When I write stories, I write them about gods and heroes – and in this story of mine, I think you're kind of a hero too.

THE HONOURS LIST

Giving a massive thanks to:

Jennifer Sutton
Ross MacBaisey
Henry Sinclair
Glenn Dove
Ganesh Subramanian Alwarappa
Jake Wilson
Joseph McLachlan
Sean Doty
Claudia May
Joanne & Nick Guy
Rebecca King
Chris Fisher
&
Charlotte Macbean

For their support and contributions to the production and publication of this book and my future projects.
You are remarkable people, and have made a young man's dream come true.

I hope to do you proud.

*To sate one's appetite, and bathe it in blood,
read on and behold…*

The
FANGS
of WAR

The Blood and Steel Saga
Book I

†

Prologue

The End Has Come

On a silent shore, in a distant land, the world was coming to an end.

Within a low-hanging mist, streams of black smoke billowed across the skyline, with ember-like orange and crimson streaked through each fold. Debris clung to the waters beneath, sloshing with the patient ripples of waves; slick mosaics of oily blood stained an otherwise pristine white beach. The lifeless flesh of the many dead bobbed among them, eyes rolling and bellies bloated like the rises of a sea serpent. It was an otherwise-pristine serenity, agonised by the scream of distant violence. That the world was coming to an end.

And yet no one seemed to know why.

Watching the thick plumes blanche the sky above, with the hollow screams of the dead and dying echoing out across the shore, a figure shrouded in shadow knelt in prayer at the water's edge, its hands opened in its lap. Water splashed across its knees; wind lashed the black cowl across its face, hiding it away from the machinations of the world. Unseeing, yet omnipresent, the figure was a fixed point in a shifting world that was slowly falling apart.

To its side, the broken boughs of a small fishing boat lay crippled across the sand. The mast had snapped clean in two, and a great gouge opened across one side to spill the goods that lay within.

Arrow points lanced its hull, splintering wood panels, with the blood-stains of fallen souls painting the vessel's interior in shades of purple and grey. It had escaped the carnage of a far-gone land with the wind still cast from its sails, carrying off the shadowy figure as fire drenched the walls of the city from which they had fled – a city lay bare by an ancient enemy and the wounds of a buried past.

The figure had cast off, gazing skyward as the mortar volleys rained down, and watched with the joy of inevitability as the world ruined itself once more. Then it faded from sight out onto the great sea, carrying the ultimate prize at its side.

The final piece of the end that would come.

In one motion, the shadow rose to its feet, turning to the thick barricade of skeletal trees that marked the shore's upper edge. With robes billowing in the sea's cold whisper, it studied the body led dormant at its feet, stirring slowly in an unconscious bliss with no recollection of the reality beyond. How poor it looked, led there: the sodden folds of red-green robes cocooning a frail body; the hunched back and twisted legs wracked with age and infirmity; the gnarled bones of arthritic fingers circling in the sand like a child; the hollow face, gaunt as a ghost, and carved with wrinkles like the bark of a tree. A half-dead man of a half-dead people, ground to dust with nothing to show for it.

Only the wretched stench of a by-gone power, its time long overdue.

As the thought came, the man seemed to stir, and a deep humanity washed over his pale features. A flutter of the eyes; the mutters of cold words through cracked lips; a twist of the face as the wind cut through from the sea. Eyes opening, blurring – the suddenness of the world rising to meet him, peering up to black-grey clouds and the haze of a delicate mist.

Into the eyes of a shadow, looming over him like a vulture.

"*Your time has come.*"

A jolt of motion; fear painted across his gaze. "Who are you? Where... where am I?"

"*I am but a servant,*" the shadow rumbled, quiet as a whisper. "*And I am here, for you.*"

"What do you mean? Who's servant?" His eyes wandered to the foamy sea to his left, and the dense swell of trees towering off to the right. "Do you have any idea who I am?"

"*It matters not, for the gods smile to you — that is why they sent me. I saved you from attack... from a death unworthy of your stature.*"

"Attacked?" A pause, trying to make sense of the sheer darkness in the shape that loomed above. "By whom?"

"*The black coats... from the north. They come with tidings of war... the heir apparent has returned to her throne. The world is coming undone as we know it.*"

"What are you saying? This doesn't make any sense. I..." His wrinkles snapped and twitched. "Who are you?"

No words followed. Silence ebbed. Only the tug of the wind dared whistle in his ears. That, and the distant voices punctuating the skies above: their screams, accompanied by the fire churning in the grey to the south.

Almost like the world was dying...

Pulling away, the shadow lifted its gloved hands to its cowl, and peeled it back slowly to reveal what lay beneath.

What came was skin, pale as dragon-fire. Brand-marks below the eyes, black and bloody like a raven's. A pale scalp like the moon, with a great trench cutting through one side like a mountain ravine. Sliding deep into the skull, through the brain itself, a rotten knot of flesh coiled within. The wound was a dislocation from all things human — it was a wound that, in all sense, would've seen any mortal man dead. And with it came the realisation that what the man lay eyes upon was not of the mortal kind and not drawing the same breath as he did. That this was no ordinary man wrought in shadow and cast from a storm. No: this was a being of the unknown, of a kind once-forgotten. A thing of blood and terror.

An arbiter at the world's end.

"What *are* you?" he muttered, the ache in his heart drawing close to giving in, beholden to the shadow figure looming high above.

"*I am a redeemer, come to pay the due of the Mother and her kind,*" it thundered, the skies seeming to swirl at its head. "*I am here to end the world as we know it so that it may be reborn again.*" A hand lingered within the robes at its side. "*And my redemption, at all accost... begins with you.*"

A blade appeared in its hand.

"*Your time has come.*"

The streaks of rust across the skyline seemed to erupt with flame; the mist curdled with the coursing wind. A screech, like the snap of branches, and a lightning blast struck through the clouds high above.

Saltwater splashed the old man's cheeks. He clutched at cold sand tainted purple by his blood. He could do nothing but pull away, his legs twisted and broken, arms little more than stumps at his sides, eyes heavy and lungs ailing and the terrifying shadow of the creature approaching at his back—

Sudden pain, exquisite across his thread-bare skull. He was dragged up from the earth by a knot of his hair with no life in his limbs left to give. Staring into the eyes of the redeemer.

The end of all things come.

With a rush of power, seething, the shadow cut across its robed body and struck the man's head from his shoulders. It was a single, swift motion of absolute demise; it was a reckless abandonment of life, as the body collapsed in a heap across the figure's steel boots and spurts of blood mixed with the sea spray.

Nothingness followed. The sky grew suddenly still, the wind but a murmur catching at the figure's ear. A blooded trophy lay in its grasp: a stump dripping blood across the sand like a tap. An end to a great many things, and a testament to the bloodshed that would follow.

The shadow cast the severed head to the sands.

"*To death, a deed is done.*"

It turned slowly, offering little more than a glance to the body at its feet, and paced slowly back to the broken boughs of the fishing boat that had brought them all that way. Its gaze drifted across the interior, skimming over the useless goods therein – catching for but a moment the dull shimmer of metal buried beneath, fallen from the robes of the man now-dead.

The shadow speared a hand within, pulling cargo aside – drawing the object into the light: an acknowledgement for the world to see.

A crown, perfectly golden in the soft glow and desperately empty in its mass. Adorned with ruby and emerald gemstones, it had ornate carvings along every spire. It held such beauty, in that quiet moment. To think of all the death it had wrought, in the end. The last remnant of an ailing nation languishing on the verge of war.

The shadow smiled. *"The King is dead."*

And the end of the world had come.

Chapter 1

Live and Let Die

They had come in the night.

They had come on the backs of brutish galleons lined with cannon and steel, coursing over the waves. They had swung down from the north, a dozen or more of them, unloading fire across the quiet walls of Casantri's harbour. There had been no warning, no sign of their coming. The sea-guard had known of the enemy only when the first steel rounds had buffeted their towers and sent them crashing down into the sea. Carnage had ensued from there; the apocalypse dashed the harbourside in grey and gold fire. Screams echoed out over the high walls, the crackle of broken ship hulls snapping through frozen winds. Still the enemy kept coming, the battle raging on through the night – and it was only when the sun mounted the shimmering waters to the east, and the plumes of smoke melded with the rising mist, that silence dared return.

In those quiet hours, those overlooking the harbourside stirred from a troubled night's rest. They opened their windows, horror etched through their skin, and looked out on the waters where the enemy had attacked.

To find it was only death that remained.

Stood on a pontoon overlooking the blood-slick waters below, General Cavara watched as a lifeless body slapped against the pillar at her feet like driftwood, the deathly-pale gaze of half-rotten eyes staring back up to her. There were many others like it nearby: bloated bodies hung limply from debris, with crows circling in their hundreds above ready take the fresh pickings. Further out in the open waters, there were the upturned hulls of ruined enemy ships led tossing as if in slumber. Several still roared with flame, pillars of smoke rising skyward to tangle with the mist and blemish an otherwise perfect blue sky.

Stood there, reeling against the pungent scent of death in her nostrils, Cavara watched the lame body beneath her for a while and sighed. It wasn't even her soldier, and it wasn't even her business, but she still had a sense that someone somewhere cared about that weird floating blob of flesh pinned to the wood under her feet. Perhaps a wife or a child or a friend. Someone, somewhere, who cared. Or maybe nobody: maybe this man had no-one to mourn them. Maybe she was the only one to look at that soggy carcass in the water and feel a touch of humanity – rather than looking upon them as just another soldier of the army, serving king and country.

Whatever that meant, anymore.

Blood spilt and an enemy defeated, Cavara hummed quietly into the wind. *Yet with so little left to show for it.*

The general turned away from the harbourside and looked back across the outer walls of Casantri, jumping between the squat houses and broad streets nestled within. Much remained unchanged in the city-proper, where even the outermost homes had remained untouched by the night's damning attack.

But, as one looked closer, the cracks began to appear. Huge slabs of stone had been reduced to shrapnel along the perimeter wall. Massive storehouses across the dockside had been burnt through and continued to smoulder in flame. Piles of rubble had appeared in the water beneath the stumpy remains of watchtowers. A blunt and bloody ruin seemed to be all that was left.

On one side of the wall, a bustling capital wallowed in its lustre and wealth – and on the other side, that same city lay with its tail between its legs, surveying the devastation of its harbour with no answers to their questions.

Cavara scoffed. *And what's the point?* She rolled her tongue and spat into the sea. *All this greatness and grandiosity... yet caught with our arse out at the first sign of danger. Dozens of our own, dead in the waters. An enemy come and gone with no answers, leaving only violence in their wake.* The body seemed to slap harder against the pillar at her feet; Cavara sighed.

What's the point?

As she turned back to the waters, lost in the depths of her thoughts, she noticed a familiar face striding along the harbourside toward her – a face that smiled her way, grinning beneath a pointed moustache.

A face that pulled an immediate bubble of sickness through her stomach, too.

Facing the open sea, a pool of dread eating at her thoughts, she tracked their approach along the pontoon behind her, marking several other soldiers also keeping pace. Her disdain grew exponentially.

As if this miserable day couldn't get any worse...

"General Cavara! Just the woman I wanted to see." He drew up alongside her, awaiting a response that never came, peering out over the waters with a curious eye. "Something interesting in the water, general? Other than the bodies and blood, that is, of course."

"No sir, nothing to see... just daydreaming," she said meekly. "That's what we're meant to do, isn't it? Pretend all this isn't real and be done with it. *'Look to the body, but not the blood spilt'*..."

"As it should be, yes." She caught his wry smile out the corner of her eye. "We'll make a general of you yet, general, if you start thinking like that."

"A kind offer sir, truly... but I think boot-polishing and arse-kissing are best left to the professionals. I wouldn't want to step on your toes."

General Revek of the First Imperial Division of Provenci screwed his nose up and spat into the water. "I think you'll find a job of such prestige holds greater power than boot polishing, general...."

"Oh, do you get to open doors for the rich too? Good for you."

"Look, if I'd come here for your childish antics, Cavara, I'd have put myself in the stocks and given you the shit to throw myself," Revek growled. "But as it so happens, that isn't the case."

"Everyone needs a past-time, sir," she mused.

"Everyone needs *respect*, too." The venom dripped from the end of his tongue, but Cavara knew the fangs would not bear: reprimanding subordinates after so much blood had been shed was a mistake not easily undone.

And you best remember it.

"So what do I owe the pleasure, general?" she said, turning to face him at last. "Have you come bearing answers as to what caused this mess?"

"Not so much what caused it," he rumbled, "but more so what we have now *lost* because of it."

She frowned. "I don't follow?"

"This information comes in the strictest confidence – and I will have you buried in a gutter before high-sun should it get out – but it was discovered this morning that the king was not in his chamber to be spoon-fed breakfast... he wasn't anywhere in the palace at all, in fact."

"So, where is he?"

General Revek inhaled at length and pulled a hand through his hair. "A contingent of the forces that attacked last night... the savages from the north... were reported to have slipped through the city walls and infiltrated the palace. And, in the confusion of the attack, they appeared to have made off with the king in one of their longboats. That may well have been the plan all along..." He clicked his tongue. "Now, this was all just hearsay to begin with, I admit. But as the king is nowhere to be found... we can assume that they were *successful* in their aims, and that our monarch is currently somewhere along the north coast... and probably not alive."

Cavara's stomach abruptly sank through the floor; the air seemed to dissipate in her lungs. Around her, the blood and bodies sweeping in with the tide didn't seem quite so serious anymore. "The king is *gone?*" the general exclaimed. "You... how has this happened? Why has any of this happened to us?"

"That's what we have yet to discover... and on that matter, that's why we're here now..."

Revek said nothing more; he twisted slightly and gestured with his hand to the soldiers at their backs.

Cavara turned, and found the limp shape of a pale man being dragged by his arms towards them. His face was a swollen rot of purple bruising, his eyes little more than tiny slits. Lacerations were carved across his chest, staining the white cloth shirt an ugly shade of pink. As he was drawn to the edge of the pontoon, sliding to his knees before them, the prisoner looked to the general with the small of his eyes, and she saw in there the pleading thoughts of a man who knew his time was up.

"We dragged him from a flagging ship capsized at the edge of the harbour," Revek exclaimed, sneering down at the poor wretch bent low at his feet. "The longboats that made off with the king used the ruined boats as cover in their retreat. We were hoping this one here knew a thing or two about that, but he has so far proven... *incapable* of offering us what we want." The foul smile reappeared. "Perhaps today he'll come to his senses...."

A wave of the hand, and the soldiers cast the prisoner to the ground. Suddenly free of restraint, they made a half-hearted attempt to scrabble towards the pontoon's edge, sliding across the wet planks.

With unassuming reflexes, however, General Revek unsheathed his sword and lunged forward to hold it at the man's neck. The prisoner ground to a sudden halt, swallowing sharply, a whimpered plea escaping his lips.

"Now where do you think you're going, hm?" Revek grinned, grabbing the prisoner by the scruff of his hair. "We aren't finished with you yet...."

Dragging him down a small flight of stairs to a platform at the water's surface, the man broke out into spasms, desperate to break free of the general's grip. He fought weakly, however, and only received a backhand across the face for his efforts.

"Now, you may have thought during the interrogation last night that I was being a bit cruel to you," Revek growled, drawing him closer, "but I can assure you I wasn't. You see, I had to provide compensation for the damage you caused to my city and my people. I had to exact pain in equal measure. So perhaps in future, it would be *wise* that you consider exactly what you're doing, attacking the most powerful coastal fortress on the western waters, expecting to get away with it unscathed. It'll save you a lot of pain, hm?" He stared into him, through him, the grey-steel pellets of his eyes pressing deep. "Because pain, you understand, can be quantified – and I intend to do *just that.*"

Cavara watched the contortion of fear on the prisoner's face. He produced little more than a strangled plea as a reply, claiming he knew nothing more.

"Oh, but you do!" Revek snapped. "You knew about the longboats... about the plan to infiltrate the palace. And I wager that you also know where the king is now. So I will listen very closely... and you will tell me *everything.*"

More unintelligible words wailed from the man's mouth. Cavara stood planted to her spot, teeth rolling against each other in agony, the soldiers at her side tapping their fingers. *This is how things are done*, came her bland and dutiful thought. *This is how things got done. This was how we get justice.*

Doesn't make it right, though—

"You lie!" Revek squawked, straining the chords in his throat. "You do know! Every one of you knew... that was why you came to this place. That was your purpose. You know... and mark my words I will bring you *misery* until you tell us what you've done..."

Striking down, Revek plunged the prisoner's face over the platform's edge into the blood-curdled water below.

An eruption of frothing pink ooze tore across the surface; hands pounded across the wood planks. From deep beneath the general's skin, veins pumped into life across his temples. He grit his teeth. The man below bucked and kicked like a startled horse, agonising as air slowly seeped from his body and the light began to fail. A hollow scream suddenly cried out from beneath the oil-slick surface.

The general grinned.

Revek drew the prisoner back to the surface, angling their face toward him. "Do you have anything you wish to say?" he barked.

The man said nothing, mumbling aimlessly, tears at the corners of his eyes—

Revek drove his head back under the water. More bubbles erupted. The prisoner's hands slapped harder against the wood like the oars of a river raft.

The head reappeared, pleading to speak its peace.

"Spit it out then," the general said.

A voice emerged all of a sudden, accented and gravelly. "The plan was to get him... as far along the coast... as possible," the man spluttered, "to have him...." The thought trailed to a close.

"What?"

"To have him killed." The prisoner shook his head. "He is most likely already dead."

Revek gave a solemn nod of confirmation, no other emotion crossing his face.

"He's actually *dead?*" Cavara exclaimed, wide-eyed with shock. "I don't understand. Why have you done this?"

"He is dead," the prisoner spat, a snarl appearing as he turned to her, "because of what your *people* have done to my homeland. Mark my words, when the Queen returns and this world bleeds again... we will come for you all—"

Revek drew his blade across and slit the man's throat, blood cascading into the waters below like a fountain. The body was released, sliding disjointedly into the scum below, life leeching from broken eyes as it sank slowly beneath the surface.

"That's enough of that," the general grumbled, sheathing his blade and rising slowly, offering a flick of his hair with all the pointless bravado he could muster. He ascended the steps, up onto the main pontoon – but found his path blocked as General Cavara stepped ahead of him, a thunder brewing in the dark of her eye.

The general frowned. "What do you want? You've heard what he said. *He's dead.* We move on. We follow procedure, and send out a search party in the coming days to retrieve the king's body. That's all there is to it… now get out of my way."

"That was not all that needed to be said, and you know it," the general challenged. "What did he mean by *'our people'* and his homeland? What was he talking about?"

"It is not your business…."

"As a general of the army seeking information after an attack on our capital, I think it is my business." Heat rose in her neck.

He scoffed. "It's on a need to know basis—"

"Look at the fucking waters, Revek!" she bellowed, spearing a finger out to the wider harbour. "Look at the dead! *Hundreds* of them. Men have *died,* because of whatever's happened in Tarraz – and that prisoner was proof. Something has happened, general, and people want answers… *I* want some answers. And as a general, I'd like to know what kind of mess the military – of which I am a *part of* – has gotten itself into." She paused, blinking slowly. "So please, go on."

The look that appeared on the general's face could've melted steel. A wave of anger bubbled there, begging to be let loose and tear Cavara's head from her neck. Begging to, and yet never being able to. Revek would catch sight of the soldiers just behind her, fear wrestling in their eyes. He would feel the ruinous weight of the general's badge against his chest-plate. He would acknowledge the unrelenting fact that procedure took precedent, and so long as the law was watching, he would have no choice but to abide.

So, without another word, Revek gestured to the two guards, who turned and paced a dozen steps back down the pontoon – leaving Cavara and the general alone at the end of the pier, the smoky mist coiling all around them like robes.

"Now, if you'd please… explain," Cavara grumbled, locking eyes with him.

Revek sighed at tremendous length, the bones clicking in his jaw. "They… *found out*," he replied cryptically.

"Found out about what?"

"The money, the corruption, the fraud… all of it. Our finely-tuned plans in Tarraz that would've made us rich… it all came to light a few nights ago." He spat into the water. "And to say the least, they were *none too happy* that we've been robbing them for the past four years under the guise of taxes, and given them nothing of any use in return…."

The wind howled around them for a moment; the sun dipped behind a column of clouds. Cavara scoffed in disbelief.

The plan… and the money was never supposed to be found. She remembered hearing about it in a report four years before, smothered in small print at the base of a new set of laws. It was an admittance, she recalled: that their control over the colony to the north – the vast former nation of Tarraz, stretching from the lowland hills of their border to the coastal fortress of Val Azbann – had eroded over the prior twenty-five years from mismanagement and neglect. It was said that the region would be ungovernable within a decade if nothing were done; that the tribes were too divided to fend for themselves. *That our exercise in arbitrary madness should come to an end,* she remembered thinking.

Yet as expected, nothing was done.

That was, until the taxes came in. Cavara scowled, recalling the arguments she had made against it. *To fund projects in the tribal lands… developments in the main cities… like a goodwill gesture from an absent father.* It had been a guise, she knew: nothing more than a false promise to cover the true purpose behind it all.

Rearmament. The word lay heavy on her tongue, slick like tar. *Military build-up. Swords and steel.*

To start the whole useless affair again…

"So the Tarrazi found out, after four years, of the inevitable," Cavara muttered, shaking her head. "Who woulda thought?"

"I know you've feel strongly about this ever since it started… and I know this also then upsets you to hear," Revek said with unusual deliberation. "But how you feel, and what you see here now, is not what's important at the moment."

"Will it ever be important, sir? To any of you?" Her voice crackled like embers, singeing her tongue. "You and your superiors were ignorant to the fact that playing games with your enemy will always end in tragedy… and what you see here, is a *tragedy*. A tragedy of ordinary people, who put faith in their king who yes, in the end, *got what he deserved*." She speared a finger out into the harbour. "Look at it, sir, and tell me whether you really believe this was all worth the few extra coin you robbed from the Tarrazi colony to fund an *invasion force…*"

"Keep your *fucking voice down* if you want to keep your damn tongue, *general*," Revek boomed, snapping suddenly. "Look, I don't *care* what you think of me or what happened. I don't care one bit that this is the cost of that decision. Soldiers are soldiers: they do, and they *die*. But I will tell you, that it is my duty to this city and its people to seek a reasonable settlement for what has happened and begin preparations for what comes next. That means that we have to deal with Tarraz and what this catastrophe means before anything else, or this will happen one hundred times over and *nothing* will change." He prodded his metallic chest-piece. "I am Head of Imperial Strategy in the Grand Council. I have managed the rearmament program for years now in secret. I am many things… but what I am *not*, is a man who's gonna stand here and pass flowers over the dead clogging the harbour. That is not my responsibility. My responsibility is to the people who live in this city and those who are willing to defend it, and that is all. Because once they are dead, they are *dead,* and died doing what they were born to do. That is all." He paused, eyes twitching. "Now, do I make myself clear on that, general?"

Cavara found the rage fight within her, but with a sigh saw it recede just as fast. *This is no argument that we need here,* came the solemn reply. *It would solve nothing in the end — only cause more grief.* She gave a single nod, once only, and met his eye with a scowl.

Not yet, at least.

"Good... I'm pleased we're in agreement." Revek's face twisted from a sour pink to a sullen grey. "You should be aware as well that there shall be a meeting of the Grand Council tomorrow to discuss any questions you may have and to work out a feasible way forward. All are expected to attend." He turned to her poignantly. "*Do not* be late."

"I wouldn't dream of it, sir," came her reply.

Cavara stood to one side and watched as Revek skulked away back towards the harbour.

"Oh, and one more thing, general," he said suddenly, twisting like a serpent to address her. "With the death of the king comes a reorganisation of leadership. Upon the king's death, it is the Imperial Commander who takes up the mantle of Governor, and the army is brought in to maintain order... and that makes me your new commanding officer." A sly grin appeared. "And I shall not hesitate in promoting those who are worthy of holding the rank of general... and ripping out those who are *not.*" A crooked glare met its mark. "And mark my words, General Cavara... I will make you suffer...."

The general turned his back to her, and Cavara watched the vulture hobble his way back towards Casantri as the walls of reality began to close in.

The king is dead. The tendons in her heart plucked like the strings of a harp. *The army takes power.* A knot of sickness ballooned in her stomach. *The dead line the waters of our capital.* Beneath her feet, the same blue-bloated body knocked against the wooden pillars.

The drums of war rise, once again.

†

Chapter 2

Where the Blood Begins

The halls and passageways of the palace were empty that morning, and the general's steel boots echoed out across the walls and spilled out of the open windows to the blue skies above. The silence, he found, was daunting; every noise was like a piercing cry. Trepidation fell taut across every doorway and coving, coursing through the halls of the palace as it did the streets outside. A mounting fear gaining there, also: a fear of what had happened, of what it all meant.

The fear of what was yet to come, and by who's hand the axe would fall.

General Revek paced the long corridor to the throne room with a deep-set premonition on his mind. *This is what we've been waiting for*, he cooed softly, the swell of air in his chest carrying him forwards through the chambers of stone blocks and finely-woven red carpets. *This is the power that has alluded us for far too long*. Across both walls, in tiny alcoves lined with ornate pillars, the domineering statues of armoured knights stood proud on their carved plinths, the red-green painted metal of their shields shimmering brightly. The general's toothy grin widened, as his eyes crossed from them to the doors at the far end.

To get what I deserve, at last.

Wedging his shoulders together, Revek heaved the doors apart with a crack of hinges, passing from a realm of light into one of swelling shadow.

Within the cold confines of the throne room, the general found himself reeling at the height of the ceiling above, supported by interlocking columns of ancient wood and a complex array of spider-webs, some as broad as sails. To his right, he found high windows blanketed in thick curtains, sealing off the midday sun entirely. And to his left, in a black-grey gloom across the far wall, he spied threadbare tapestries rippling softly in the dark, depicting the tales of long-past glories in threads of gold and green.

Revek found his nose curl at the sight of them, a wrinkle of disgust coiling in his mind. *Former glories, left to grow tired in the shadows.* Glories he had been told as a child; taught in military camps as a junior; studied in field guides as a general and then general. *Watching, all the while, as those self-same glories fell to rubble, at the hand of an impotent king with one foot in the grave.* The concessions; the treaties signed; the lies of prosperity as the vaults were run into the ground. *And now the old fool lies dead, without responsibility or concern, and the nation is in turmoil.* He ground his teeth, sighed gracelessly into the void. *And now we're left to pick up the pieces.* The grin reappeared – at that moment, his eyes turned to the back of the room.

And here to serve its new leader.

The first thing the general came to, was a high-backed throne of oak darker than any he had ever seen, with carved rings curling out at its edge like rolling waves. Before it, a crimson mass of silk and fur spilt over the tiles like an open wound, rising over the arm of the chair and snaking out of sight behind the massive bear-like form of a man. Donned in a hulking suit of armour, with the traumatising gaze of heavy grey pupils sunk deep into his skull, Revek was entirely captivated by the figure. A man he knew he should hold no fear of, for they had been colleagues of the army for near a decade – yet who, sat in that massive oak throne within a veil of shadow, the general found himself short of breath and weak at the legs in the presence of, only mounting enough courage to grace him with a bow at the last moment.

"Supreme Governor Alvarez," Revek said.

"General Revek," the man on the throne boomed. "About time you and I talked again. Please, stand."

Revek rose to full height, the unbroken gaze of the new Governor holding him once more. "You wanted to speak with me?"

"Yes. On a few matters, in fact." The bear-man rose from his seat to a ferociously intimidating height, the throne little more than a stool at his back by comparison. "How fares our army, general? I'm sure you've addressed them all by now…"

Revek bristled – *they are* my *army* – but said nothing of it. "In good spirits, sir," he replied. "They were pleased with the result last night, and at the enemy slain, even with the loss of life."

"This is good… very good."

"Although we will need to try and recover as many vessels as we can and get them to the dockyards in the next few days. We took some heavy casualties when they first attacked and many of our ships lay beleaguered up the coast."

"Do what you must, general. I entrust your judgement to see these things tended to."

"Thank you, sir."

"Hm."

Revek found a coldness in his chest, as the Governor's face twisted into a look of disgust. The general, suddenly afraid, wondered if he had wronged the man on some matter, or if there was something he had said—

"The matters I wished to discuss with you," Alvarez rumbled abruptly, "are highly sensitive… I hope you know that."

Revek snapped back to attention. "Of course, sir."

"Because they concern communication we've had directly with our informants in Tarraz."

The edge of his mouth twitched. "Shouldn't that information come to *me* to report to *you*, as commanding officer?"

"When we formalise power, yes." A warning glance shot his way.

"Remember, the masses don't know what's happened yet. They don't know I sit on the throne, or that I draw the sword and sign the laws. They don't know you are now my second-in-command. And, to control the changeover of power successfully – without starting a miserable *bloody* rebellion – we must keep things as they were for now." He arced a finger back towards the throne. "As far as is concerned, the king still sits in that chair, rotting his way to oblivion, until we address the full council tomorrow. Are we at an understanding about that?"

Revek ground his teeth. "Completely, sir."

"Good. Now, to the matter at hand…" With a huge paw, Alvarez reached within the folds of his robe and plucked a folded wedge of paper out, handing it to Revek to read. "We received this from a scout in the early hours of this morning, amidst the fighting. It came straight from Tarraz… poor bastard had to dodge crossbow fire just to get over the border. It's a mess if I've ever seen one."

And that's no underestimation, Revek thought, studying the scrawled ink across the page in his hands, blotches of rainwater and blood splattering like blisters at the edges. He recited every part as it came, and found each to be more damning than the last. '*A gross loss of life, as hundreds of Provenci officials are publicly executed in the Tarraz capital*'… '*what seems to be a nation-wide revolution against the puppet government*'… '*tribes have come together to form a new leadership, led by an unknown*'… '*all other diplomats have been expelled*'… '*borders have been reinforced and closed off*'… '*an old enemy has returned*'. A bubble ballooned in his throat; Revek found no words would come. The corruption had been unravelled, and the country had erupted into revolution right on their doorstep overnight. Then they had manned the oars, attacked Casantri by sea, infiltrated the palace and kidnapped their dying king as revenge. A demonstrable act of treason; anarchy and humiliation of the highest order. Reading on, it was the last line that held the general's gaze the longest.

'*We have lost control*'.

"Quite the read, isn't it?" Alvarez said, sighing. "The fucking *savages.*"

Revek was still found wanting for a reply. "It's anarchy…"

"It's more than anarchy. They've ripped up everything we've worked to secure for *twenty-five years* and bathed it in blood. I always knew those foul creatures and their backward morals couldn't be trusted… and here we are. Caught as bystanders, watching our vassal state tear itself to pieces. It's more than anarchy, general. It's *chaos.*"

Revek withdrew the letter. "Does it pose a military threat?"

"They shelled our harbour and killed dozens of our soldiers, general – yes it is a *military threat.*"

"Beyond an act of revenge, I mean."

Alvarez seemed to stiffen. "Do you mean to suggest that what happened last night goes *unchallenged*?" he said coldly.

"Not at all, sir. I simply… looking at it militarily… would question whether there may be any further attack. That would decide whether we man the borders and double the guard, or kick the bastards in the teeth for what they've done." Revek tried to recover more ground. "It um… this report says nothing about border *raids*, you see, only *reinforcement* of border towns—"

"Reinforcement is a precursor to aggression. Why reinforce a border if you didn't intend to invade?"

"Because we may want to take back what's ours."

"We will take back what is rightfully ours, general. Don't play games about that." There was a wild glint in the Supreme Governor's eyes then – the look of a starving predator, baying for blood, finally laying eyes on its prey for the first time. A look that spoke volumes of the bloodshed that would undoubtedly come. "This is no simple sleight, general. Treat *everything* as a military threat. Take no chances on that. No one attacks the greatest nation of the Icebreaker Sea and gets away with it. *No-one.*"

Revek nodded once, once only. "Aye… sir."

A few moments passed, moments more, as Revek watched the dark machinations smooth over in the Governor's eye. Whatever had overcome him, and run with uncontrolled anger through his mind, subsided as fast as it had come. Alvarez rolled his tongue across the roof of his mouth and exhaled loudly through his nose.

"Did you get anything else out of that prisoner we dragged off the burning ship?" he enquired suddenly, lifting his gaze again. "Did he know anything of the king's whereabouts?"

"We didn't get anything out of him last night. So I took him to the harbourside this morning to… *test the water*, shall we say." Revek grinned, relishing the memory. "It certainly got him talking."

"And?"

"And the attack last night had no intention of succeeding. From his explanation, it was more of a distraction so they could infiltrate the palace and make off with their cargo in the chaos."

"That's an awful waste of life and ships to achieve so little."

"I believe that was their intention, sir… to achieve their ultimate goal no matter the cost."

"Barbaric…" The word echoed through the chamber like a drumbeat. "Did he say anything more?"

"The prisoner explained that they intended to seize the king from the palace and take him along the coast to the north… to find a quiet bay, and…"

"And what, general?"

"… and execute him, sir."

"Well…" The bear-man nodded, looking surprised – but with the corners of his mouth twitching upwards with every second that passed. "Isn't that a *shame*."

"Yes sir… truly, a *shame*."

"Then it is confirmed… the king is dead, and he has died at the hands of the Tarrazi savages: those who dare stand against us, and rally their forces, and attack us with such violent disregard." A single nod; a set of pearlescent white teeth shimmering in the low light. "An act of *war*, no doubt."

"Without question sir," the general beamed.

"That being the case, we must yet proceed with caution. With the king's untimely demise, the last thing we want is carnage in the streets. We need to see off his death tactfully…"

"A palace funeral, perhaps, sir?"

"Nothing of the sort," Alvarez spat.

Revek swallowed. "Of course."

"We will find the body, wherever it may be, and we shall let the masses see their dead king and be done with it. He's gone now, and war beckons… whatever legacy he demands of himself matters nought now." A pause. "Not that I'd ever tempt it anyway…"

"Excellent, sir."

"I would like you to organise the search party. I want two generals and a handful of men, on whatever ships we can spare, heading north in two days to retrieve the body." Another pause. "In fact, let that General Cavara lead it. I feel she's up to the job."

She deserves nothing of the sort. "Of course, sir."

The Governor wagged a finger his way. "Don't squabble over it, either. I know you two have your differences."

I hope she dies. "Wouldn't dream of it, sir."

"Good." Alvarez turned to the throne, gazing up at the vast curtains draped behind it. "Now, I must beg your leave, general. The Mother has summoned me to her counsel…"

"Of course." He bowed, not sure who to, and turned hastily towards the doors, hoping to escape the awkward confines as fast as he could, as if the weight of the world were bearing down—

"Oh, and general?"

Revek stopped and swore under his breath; he turned to face him.

"Ready the men to march within the coming days," he said gravely. "Casantri does not kneel to the whim of *savages*."

Revek gave an exaggerated bow, a curling smile like a crescent moon gracing his thin face. "I shall see to it immediately, sir… hail to Provenci."

He turned back to the door.

And hail to me.

†

Chapter 3

Do Not Speak Their Name

The doors fell closed with a shudder of metal. Alvarez stood alone in the vastness of the throne room, with only the shadows dancing across the walls to keep him company. To his side, he heard the faint ripples of civilisation drift up to knock against the panes of the palace windows, detailing in their tiny sounds the hive of activity that flourished across the vastness of Casantri below. The great capital of imperial power, grown tired in its old age. The former kingdom that now lay in his grasp.

The first thunder of the coming storm.

So it begins. He nodded slowly. *The imperial army, come to power.* A roll of the shoulders; a click of the tongue. *A new Governor, set to rule.* Spinning on his heel, Alvarez turned towards the throne and gazed up to the black curtains that lay sealed shut behind it.

The Mother herself, calling to her new champion.

He had heard the stories, told in the barracks when he had been but a young palace guard: tales of the god-like beings who inhabited the capitals of the four nations of the Icebreaker Sea, known as the Mothers. Secretive, unforeseen deities, seeking counsel exclusively with a nation's ruler as they had done for millennia before. He recalled almost reminiscently the tales of how, if any tried to access the Mother's counsel beyond the chosen leader, they were never seen or heard from again. How curious soldiers made fools themselves, entering the chamber like mischievous children and never coming out again. There were many rumours as to what happened to those unworthy of entering that chamber, but whenever he heard them Alvarez simply shook his head and smiled. For he knew that the Mothers acted merely as a conduit to greater knowledge – that they represented the only point of access to a greater being, unseen and yet always present. The one who lay shrouded in legend, said to live at the heart of the Icebreaker Sea. The one who commanded all things and controlled the balance of the world.

The All-Mother herself.

As the thought came, and he gazed up at the broad curtained veil where the Mother was said to reside, he found a whispering voice rise and fall patiently in the base of his skull. For several days it had called to him, at first little more than a faint hum, but since that morning he had found its tune grow sharper, as if reciting a melody in an ancient tongue that was completely lost on him. It was a summoning, he knew – Her summoning, although before that day there had been no purpose behind its subtle sweet song.

But if the king is dead, and the leadership has passed onto me, he mused with a searching eye, *then the summons are to her next champion.* That as the city recoiled from a vicious attack, and the throne lay empty once more, the Mother had cast her gaze out to who came next.

And it is I she found, stood waiting.

He knelt before the throne, eyes closing, the thrum of the Mother's cry echoing out through his ears.

"*Proveto densi anis, priventi ata tori,*" he muttered, the dead language rolling poetically over his tongue. "I answer the call of the Mother; may my fate rest in her hands."

With an abruptness that hit with the impact of falling stone, the call in the base of his skull was suddenly extinguished, and a wave of pain struck through his spine like a snapping blade. The room fell dark around him; the ceiling spun and his eyes twitched like a breaching dam. Every fibre in his system convulsed, fighting the subconscious as it drew slowly back into the shadows. Trying with every ounce to keep awake.

Or perhaps, trying to stay alive.

In the expanse before him, a shadow lunged suddenly from the beyond the curtained veil, swelling outwards into a revolving cloud of dust and dark matter, arcing overhead in an impossibly-black swirl.

Alvarez slipped back and fell across the stone at his feet. Coldness ruptured within him, crystallising in his veins, puncturing his soul like a knife. It was all-encompassing, eclipsing every bead of light that dared enter the chamber, swallowing the life from the world as his vision cleared and he swayed laboriously to his feet.

"Mother Katastro…" he muttered breathlessly.

"*Child*," a voice boomed from the vortex above, reverberating through his eardrums like the tiny cracks of bell-chimes. "*I've been waiting for you for some time now.*"

"For some time, Mother?"

"*Yes, child. It is fate which brought you here… and it is fate alone that dictates where you are now.*"

"I don't follow, Mother… if you could—"

"*Alvarez.*" The sound of his name on her voice conjured a breach of sickness in his stomach. "*So dutiful, yet so naïve… always lusting for power. These things, the king was not.*"

"'*Was not*', Mother? So it is true?"

"*It is true. The king is dead… as destiny foretold.*"

Alvarez frowned. "He knew that he would die?"

"*All who rule shall know their fate… such is as destiny permits. The king knew, but simply chose never to believe.*" A silence; the shadow swelled above him. "*I would hope you are not like him, child… for fate is a cruel mistress, but also an undeniable truth. Whether one likes it… or not.*"

"I would not dream of it, Mother—"

"*For I come to you not with the good tidings I have otherwise met with your forebears — there are… a great many things wrong in the world, that must take precedent at this time.*"

Alvarez nodded with concern. "Do you speak of the war, Mother?"

A long, punishing silence, ebbing out into the void. The shadow held no gaze, yet he found its eyes gouge into him then. *"I speak of the end times, child,"* it thundered eventually. *"I speak of the end times for us all."*

"What do you mean by *'us all'?* What is happening?"

"The balance of the world is breaking, child. Our power, residing with the All-Mother… I sense it is failing. We have not heard her commands for many nights now."

"What does that mean?"

Another grave pause. *"It means she has passed, my child… and with her gone I fear I, like my sisters, shall follow."*

An unusual weight doused the Mother's voice as it caught in his ear, something verging on sorrow. Alvarez looked up and into the vortex above, dancing from shadow to shadow, and found the floor seemed to fall away at his feet. That war was coming, and the end times were upon them.

And the Mother is dying before me, and there is nothing I can do.

"You cannot *die*!" the Governor spat. "I need to know, I… I need you. This nation, *our people*, need you. We are on the brink of war, an enemy on our doorstep… you cannot *die* and leave us to slaughter—"

"This nation needs leadership," the voice growled, a snap like a crackling storm arcing through the chamber above. *"It needs strength, virtue, courage. It does not need me. I am a vassal of the All-Mother. I can see destiny, and what the future entails. I am but a soothe-sayer… you, and you alone, are this nation's leader. Not me."*

Emboldened by her words, Alvarez tamed the anxiety in his chest and exhaled at length. "Then what must I do, Mother? What must I do, if you are to die… to save all this? To keep my *power?*"

The void snapped before him – he almost made out a smile.

"You must seize it."

"What does that mean?"

"You have power, yes, but you have yet no strength… no blood to your steel or bite to your command. It is not yours to keep this power you possess…

it is yours to take it, to feed that urge which you so desire."

A glimmer of blood-fuelled pride swelled in his heart. "So I am to go to war then?"

"To war, my child… your destiny lies in Tarraz. It is there you shall find this power you so long for."

"There is nothing in Tarraz, Mother. Nothing but brutes and savages… creatures of a bygone age who need correction. There is nothing but worthless blood and reforged glory in that land—"

"So bold, yet so naïve," the voice tempted as it lurched closer. *"You know that is not true, deep inside. You know what awaits you in that land."* A pause, as if it were studying him. *"You've known for twenty-five years… what lies waiting for you in Tarraz…"*

"You know *nothing* of that," Alvarez spat, a furnace roaring through his system suddenly.

"I know all, my child, for I am the Mother of destiny and will… you just fear the reality that brings—"

"She is *dead.*"

"It is not so."

"I saw it with my own eyes. I saw her cast from that wretched cliff in the midst of battle, a sword through her stomach—"

"… escaped into the mountains, has lived in exile all these years… you know it's true." The shadow swung gently backwards, up towards the curtains again. *"You fed lies to your superiors back then,"* it continued, *"and now that you hold the reins of power you still feed those same lies to yourself. Destiny has foretold that she lives… and that the rise of Tarraz shall come again."*

Alvarez struck a finger out toward the void. "You *lie.*"

"I am the Mother of destiny and will—"

"I scoff at it – this is lies."

"This is the truth… fate, as the prophecy foretold."

"To hell with your fucking *prophecy*…"

"You cannot abandon destiny—"

"I am master of my own destiny!" Alvarez roared. Spittle flew from his mouth, his voice crackling with anger. Rage boiled like a tempest in the rounds of his eyes, flaring red fire through his mind. "This is my power, and this is my will… you said it yourself: I am the ruler here, *not* you. Do not distort that with your lies and this ruinous fallacy that that bitch still lives. She is *dead*… twenty-five years stand as testament. Do not dare offer any pretence otherwise… this destiny is mine and mine *alone*."

The shadow shifted slowly, slipping back towards the curtained veil. Silence ebbed; the anger rattling through his bones but found no direction to exert its force. The Mother loomed large ahead, uncaring, a master of a world that fell apart all around it. He was but a mortal, in the end.

"Whatever you claim to control," it rumbled slowly, shaking the dust from the walls, *"does not matter. The Iron Queen of Tarraz yet lives…"*

In a sudden explosion of shadow, the figment slipped through the veil; the curtains fell still.

"And destiny shall prevail."

†

Chapter 4

It Comes From the North

It took a good few tugs to prize Savanta's axe from the man's skull, blood cascading from the wound as she tore her slippery hands away and took a draw of cold air. It was cold on the plains that afternoon, with a biting wind pulling down from the mountains. But she didn't even have time to register, let alone time to care, before the next brute charged at her, steel swinging wildly in his hand.

She dived to the left, swung right, clattered against the man's breast-plate mid-stride. A short-sword turned for her: her axe handle knocked it aside, using the blunt end to jab at the man's face. It poked him in the eye, forcing him to stumble. She swung the axe again, this time hitting home, connecting with flesh and bone as she severed the forearm in two and sent the hand spinning off into the grass. Colour left the brute's face; she had never seen an uglier shade of white. Another swing and she cleaved him across his throat. A jet of blood arched through the sky like a fountain; the man's wretched eyes rolled to the back of his head. He collapsed moments later.

And even before he had hit the floor, Savanta was already turning and running, eyes wild and hungry in search of her next kill.

In the open stretches of the Provenci plains sprawling out before her, sparse pockets of trees formed here and there, where the enemy were stretched thin but still charging on. Even as she scanned the near horizon, there were already more bearded figures in thick metal plates storming into the tree-line to her left, where fighting still seized through the shadows like spasms of flame. A whisper of a smile caught her face.

It looks to be a good day after all.

Savanta made for the trees, where the clatter of metal and the screams of the dying echoed all around. More of her people came into view, the red and green sash across their shoulders rippling in the light winds. A few were scattered in the bushes to her left locked in bitter fighting. To her right, more of the enemy came into view between the trees, some she found armed with the thin wooden shapes of crossbows. As the realisation came, one let fly a piercing bolt that whistled through the low-lying branches just next to her, and pierced one of her men in the mouth, shattering his jaw.

He hit the mud moments later.

Savanta ground her teeth, and charged for the firing line. A few suddenly-fearful faces turned to her, readying weapons and firearms.

A bolt let fly and Savanta sidestepped, twisting to watch the tiny metal ball barrel past her chest. A second snapped against her axe-blade, the debris impaling a nearby tree. A third, fumbled in the hands of a younger man, crackling through the branches above her head. A fourth—

Found an axe in his skull before the crossbow snapped, a last silent breath drawn on blooded lips.

Aware of the others around her, Savanta dodged another shot and reclaimed her axe, stodgy pink brain-matter still wedged along the blade as she circled back round. Another swing and she cracked a man's crossbow down the middle, draw wire snapping against her bared and bloodied hand. She hissed with the sudden pain – the man stumbled back, defenceless, as Savanta swung again, ever intent to kill, to strike another on her tally of a good day's work—

Another blade slid through, knocking aside her weapon as she spun on her heel, spitting and wild-eyed and—

Staring into the eyes of a titan-like figure fastened knee-to-neck in metal plates, face awash with black paint and thick scars, grinning like a butcher set to slaughter.

Savanta gasped; struck out fearfully. The huge figure snapped it aside with his own weapon as if it were little more than a strand of grass. Lunging forward, she shrieked as his massive hand coiled around the back of her head and snagged a huge knot of her hair.

She didn't even have time to register, let alone time to care, before the huge man lurched forward and smashed his head through the bridge of her nose.

A shot of pain blanketed her face, fuzzing and swelling as her eyes spun, the forest before her fading and forming with each blink. Suddenly she was falling back, landing across the leaf-litter below. Blood leaked across her mouth, bitter on her tongue. She spat, watched it land on the boot of the butcher who'd put her there, and looked up to see a blade falling towards her and the mad lust in his eyes.

So much for all the hard work—

A glint of metal like a shooting star, and an arrow rifled through the man's shoulder before the blade had a chance to move. He squealed like a pig, pulling away, reaching for the shaft now embedded in his collar.

Sensing the opportunity as the man reeled with agony, Savanta flicked a knife from her waist and propelled herself to her feet, spearing upwards towards the canopy—

The knife lodging up through the man's jaw.

Blood exploded from his artery, streaming down the blade and across Savanta's arm. His eyes seemed to ignite for a moment, the man's huge paws scrabbling for the hilt as life slipped away.

When Savanta finally let go, the mass of muscle sagged to the ground and buckled into the mud like a felled tree. Silence suddenly ebbed out through the forest grove, the clash of steel drawing to an end, a grand symphony of bloodshed meeting its final moments. Looking out to the faces of her people beyond the trees, Savanta took a long draw of cool air and sighed at great length.

Only to find a bubble of blood pop in her nose and a sudden twinge of pain emanating therein, as she ground her teeth and rolled her eyes and screamed out into the green.

"How'd you manage that?"

They had taken shelter around the base of a great oak tree, where shafts of the mid-afternoon sun struck through breaches in the canopy above. A few of her fellow scouts were busy recovering the dead nearby and finding them places to be buried; others prepped their weapons, cleaning them and sharpening them with whetstones; a handful sat tending their wounds along the northern edge of the woods, at the invisible line that marked the border between Provenci and the southernly reaches of Tarraz. The invisible line they had been tasked to guard until they're dying breath.

And for many that day, that had been just the case.

"It was an unfortunate incident," Savanta replied, pinching the bridge of her nose and spitting into the earth, "between a large man's forehead and my face... an incident where, by some miracle, I actually came off better."

Markus, her second-in-command, gave a wry smile. He was twice her age, greying around the edges with deeply wrinkled cheeks and mellow brown eyes. "I can see that," he mused, studying the blooded swell. "Although, I don't know that I've ever seen someone's nose grow *inside* their skull before."

"Fuck yourself," she scoffed, but couldn't help but laugh too. They had worked together for nearly a decade: from a small cohort of mercenaries roving the countryside for trouble, into a scouting company of the imperial army organised to defend against enemy raids. They had been side by side, through sweat and steel and dirt and blood, for most of her life. And now, looking into the jovial, conciliatory gaze of Markus then, she saw there a weathered face of a dutiful, honest man – the face, too, of her oldest friend.

"Don't think you'll be able to smell with that thing much

anymore," Markus added. "Not that there's much to smell around here, that is, besides damp leather and mud."

Savanta released the pressure on the bridge of her nose and found, with some satisfaction, that the blood flow had stopped. "I fear much the same... although we did well today, I'd wager. How many were lost in the fight?"

"Of our number, the last count was six... although considering the enemy totalled near three dozen, I'd say we had a very good day indeed."

"Wish my nose could say the same..."

"Don't fret, you'll recover... you might look even more like a troll than you already do, but I'm sure you'll manage."

"Fuck yourself."

"You're very welcome," he said with a warm smile. "Speaking of trolls, do you remember the last time *I* got an injury like that? About a year or so back along the eastern hills..."

She pondered. "Vaguely, something about that..."

The greying man clasped his hands, reminiscing the tale. "We were sent in to clear out a troll that had been terrorising local farms and breaking their mills – so we found that cave under the waterfall where it was said to have lived. And I went in... assuming it would only be about four foot tall and no great bother... and—"

"Got hit across the stomach with a club the size of a small building," Savanta finished, shaking her head at the memory. "Yes, I do recall. And I remember it because you were *insufferable* for days on end after."

"I had just been hit with a club the size of a small building, mind," Markus scoffed. "Not only that, but I also had a gouge across my stomach big enough to mine from... still got the scar, come to think of it."

"It's not a bad thing... what is life without brushing shoulders with imminent death?"

"Wouldn't fancy an easy life?"

She screwed her nose up. "What, as some housemaid in a grand estate, or a local baker cooking fresh bread for the young? Over my *dead body* would I."

"Well, it nearly was... had my arrow not intervened."

"Yea... I was meaning to thank you for that. It would've been quite an unsatisfactory way to die."

"Is that so?" He nodded sarcastically. "And what would be a good way for the great Savanta to greet the gods, then?"

She looked to him with contentment in her gaze. "That when I die, I will get to look the bastard in the eye and know for a fact that, at that moment, I am staring down the devil himself..."

Markus smirked. "For nothing else will suffice?"

She smiled back. "Nothing else will suffice—"

"Captain!"

The voice came from ahead of her. Savanta shifted her gaze between the nearest trees and found one of her scouts approaching, stumbling through the grove with a sweat-streaked face.

"Aye?" she called.

"We've found something... ma'am," the scout spluttered.

"Found *what?*"

"People, ma'am... lots of them. Coming from Tarraz—"

Savanta was on her feet and moving before the scout had a chance to finish.

"What am I looking at here?"

Squinting through the spyglass, Savanta traced the horizon and tried to make sense of the shifting black mass that had manifested there. Like an ant colony, it seemed to swarm over the grassland in tight clusters, weaving in and out of each other in some pattern that she found impossible to follow.

"They appeared as the fighting ended, ma'am," the scout explained. "The bulk of the force has remained in place, but we've tracked several small groups breaking off to the east and west. The scouts have been ordered to watch our flanks and remain hidden in the scrub. We don't wanna be snuck up on out here…"

No, we do not…

As the scout spoke, Savanta tracked one of the small clusters of soldiers as they peeled off from the main hive, marching left across the plain. They seemed different than the others at the centre: their armour was lighter, and they carried large sacks across their backs with tools poking out the top like spears. Their motions were purposeful, highly disciplined: as if there were a place to go and a job to do. She questioned why, and what they intended to do, but when several heavily-laden carts emerged from the central mass and followed their path just behind, a ball of thread began to unravel in the back of her mind.

"They have building supplies… although I somewhat doubt they're building houses," she exclaimed, retracting the spyglass and lying it at her side.

"What could they be doing?" Markus asked to her right, stationed with his own spyglass.

"It could be anything… but with that kind of military presence, and that quantity of material being carted to the border, whatever it is will be within our jurisdiction." She rolled her tongue. "And it doesn't look good by any stretch of the imagination…"

"What do you advise?"

She gave a long pause. "We have to warn the capital."

"But the capital's been attacked," the scout queried. "You saw the reports… why would they waste personnel coming all the way out here just to keep an eye out? Surely that's our job?"

"Our *job,* is to patrol the border and stop raids… *not* to count the heads of a Tarrazi army and assess if it's a precursor to war." The final word drew a few concerned looks at her back. "Because as much as I love cutting down ugly bastards with a hatchet for a living, we ain't the soldiering type… and we ain't about to start now."

"What shall we do, then, ma'am?"

She drew a hand through her hair. "We scout out this area for a good place to make camp and feed regular reports to the capital about what we've found. But we leave *nothing* to chance, alright? If they spot us and start charging, we run. Because we are scouts... not soldiers."

A few murmurs came as a response, as the realisation of what lay before them began to kick in.

"Good, I'm glad we're in agreement... scout?" The woman next to her met her eye. "Send a message to Casantri. Tell them what's happening here and what our plan of action is. Say we await further orders." Savanta pulled closer. "And don't mess this up, or the entire north will descend upon us with fire and hell and we'll be nothing but ruins in weeks. Understood?"

The scout said nothing, as she got to her feet and ambled off into the forest back towards the capital, an expression of terror wearing heavy across her face. Savanta smiled.

No pressure.

9 781399 962261